SPIRIT WALKER
Rise Of The Thunderbird

D. D. Morrow

SPIRIT WALKER
Rise Of The Thunderbird

Charleston, SC
www.PalmettoPublishing.com

Spirit Walker: Rise Of The Thunderbird

First Edition

Hardcover ISBN: 978-1-63837-644-6
Paperback ISBN: 978-1-63837-645-3
eBook ISBN: 978-1-63837-646-0

FROM THE ENCYCLOPEDIA, AND MY TAKE

Native American beliefs are what Indians used to or, in some cases, still believe that the spirit power could be gained by certain people through certain ceremonies. The power may be centered in some animals, areas, or things, making them powerful or dangerous. Some tribes had a name for the spirit power. The Sioux referred to it as Wakonda. Some tribes believed in a great spirit an especially powerful god. But the great god belief was always accompanied by a belief in many other spirits or in the general spirit power. The peoples of Middle America and the Andes, for example, worshiped hundreds of gods. The Inca believed that their ruler was also a god. A god king, and they worshiped him with their many other gods. The Indian's in some areas greatly feared the ghost of the dead. But few Indian's gave much thought to life after death or an idea of heaven. **The Guardian Spirit**- One way of reaching the powerful spirit world was through a personal spiritual helper called a guardian spirit. When boys and, in some cases, girls reached their teens, they went through an initiation ceremony to help them find their guardian spirit, a vision quest. Shamans believe in the spirit world.

CONTENTS

PROLOGUE

Bayfield, CO.—The Fighting Cranes trailed by two goals at halftime after allowing three goals in the final three minutes of the first half.

The Fighting Cranes, however, were not going to be denied.

Looking to reach the district championship game for the first time in its history, the Bayfield girls lacrosse team dominated the second half en route to a 17-10 victory over Adobe High School on Tuesday night in the semifinals of the Class 1A, District 5 tournament at Legion Field.

"This is so exciting, so exciting." said senior co-captain Nakoma Standing Elk, who was the Fighting Crane's 2020 player of the year. "Our team has worked so hard to get to this point really, really hard to get to this point. I'm so proud of every girl here. I can definitely see from us being a new team my freshman year to us going to district finals as a senior, we've come so far and I'm so proud of everyone."

CHAPTER 1

DREAMS OR VISION

Nakoma Standing Elk is in her senior year of high school. She attends in the small town of Bayfield, CO. Just northeast of the Ute Indian reservation where she lives with her mother Mary and father Johnathon. Nakoma is five foot six and weighs about one hundred and ten pounds. She has a solid athletic body. Her hair is black and long, hanging down past her calves. Her skin is of a dark tan and brown eyes.

The farm they live on was small in comparison to most of only a hundred acres. Her father raised 300 head of cattle and grew hay for the other portion of the fields. Her mother was a home maker and made sure that the family needs were met. Nakoma was a well-mannered child in respects to her parents, but she had plans of her own.

She sought to become an archaeologist and venture the world of historical finds. Her father on the other hand was old fashioned in his thinking and traditional in the native American ways. He was never pleased in her life's ambitions, thinking more that her place was on the Res.

She was a straight A student athlete. She volunteered time at the reservation stables, aside from her lacrosse practices and games. This time of her senior year her father had pushed for her to take the vision quest of their ancestors.

The night the girls won the state championship. Nakoma was tired as she arrived home with her mom and dad at the ranch. Knowing that tomorrow would be another long day, she washed up and went to bed with her window cracked to allow the breeze to come through. The curtains gave a small wave as they danced with the night air. At around two in the morning, a dream consumed her; Nakoma had been having the same recurring dream since she was thirteen. She could see herself as she was younger than she was now. She could see that they were memories of her childhood. Nakoma watched herself, seeing a time when she was eight years old and remembering how she played in the meadow behind her grandparents' house. Birds would come and land on her shoulders, singing as she walked through the tall grass; her arms stretched wide, feeling the grass between her fingers.

Then she could see the row of trees that ran along a stream on the back side of the property. Now, Nakoma was older at the age of twelve. She remembered she would go there and stand at the stream with a handful of bird seed that she stole from her grandmother's bird feeders. She recalled that when she was smaller, she would take a broom handle and tip the feeder over till it spilled the seed on the ground. Her grandmother would yell at her, chasing her off, but Nakoma would just laugh and run away to the stream. At the stream, she would sit as chipmunks, squirrels, and even deer would come take the seed from her hands.

Nakoma then crossed the stream and came to a field of gold. She was now her current age, seventeen. She was also no longer watching herself but seeing everything firsthand. She walked through the field even though she did not recognize where she was. She did know that the wheat was almost ready for harvest. Nakoma came to a small clearing in the field, where it looked like deer would come and lie down for the night. The wheat was all pressed down, kind of like a small crop circle about twenty feet in diameter. Just then a deer came into the clearing with her. He was massive and one of the most beautiful bucks she'd had ever seen. He was a magnificent buck, with a rack that was as wide as she was tall. He had at least forty points as the deer made his way to her. He held his head up high as he came before Nakoma. Then he seemed to bow giving Nakoma the privilege of petting him.

Nakoma stood and smiled for a moment in awe of this magnificent creature. Then she reached out her hand to touch the deer. Suddenly a bolt of lightning struck the ground next to them, and thunder shook all around. The deer was gone running as fast it could. Dark clouds began to cover the sky turning the day into night. It was like someone turned off a light switch. Lightning struck again behind Nakoma, this time starting a fire in the field around her. Smoke began to fill the air, and Nakoma began to cough, breathing in the smoke. Lightning struck harder this time knocking Nakoma off her feet. Nakoma was scared as smoke and fire surrounded her, causing her to cough even more and her eyes to burn.

Then something large flew in, swooping past Nakoma as she was trying to get back up. The wind from the creature sent her back onto the ground. Nakoma was now scrambling to get to her feet. She could see that the circle she was in, is now about sixty feet across, with fire and smoke all around.

Nakoma began to cry for help, still coughing from the smoke. Suddenly, a large gust of wind came in again. Nakoma shielded her face with her left arm and planted her feet. She was still pushed back as a large winged humanoid creature landed about twenty feet from her. His head was like that of a bird, his body of a man. His huge wings were raised high. His legs were like that of an eagle. Nakoma's stomach began to turn now, as the creature then threw its hands out to both sides and gave a gut-wrenching screech. Thunder shook and lightning filled the skies once again, and Nakoma began to scream.

"Nakoma honey are you alright? "Her mother asked turning on the bedroom light with her father right behind holding a double-barreled shotgun and scanning the room.

"What is it? "Her father said in a deep stern manly voice ready to shoot whatever moved. Just then the family cat rubbed up against his leg, causing him to jump. "Damn it Bob!" Bob was the family cat, and he had no tail hence the name Bob. But he was a good-looking calico, and definitely fat. You could tell he never missed a meal. Bob ran between her father's legs again, causing her father to lightly kick him away. Nakoma's mother sat on the edge of the bed and hugged her.

4

"Is everything okay?" Mary asked giving her a kiss on top of the head.

"I was in this field with a deer, and then this thunder and lightning started a fire around me. There was so much smoke, then this large bird creature." Nakoma was cut short in her explanation of her dream as her father interrupted in anger.

"A dream, really Nakoma? At your age! You're seventeen!" Johnathon scolded throwing his left hand in the air with disgust.

"Johnathon Standing Elk, you take that back!" Mary shot back, giving him a glare that said she could kill him right now. Then she turned back to Nakoma.

"It's okay dear. We know you have a lot going on right now. Your senior year coming to an end so quickly, colleges to go see, your work at the stables."

"She needs to get ready for her vision quest, that's in two weeks. That's important!" Johnathon scolded, pointing his finger in their direction.

"John, we decided it was her choice, not ours." Mary said as Johnathon gave an agitated expression turning toward the door of the room.

"Mom, Dad, I want to go to college. I've got three full ride scholarships from three really good universities, and yes the vision quest is important to our heritage." Nakoma said to them, leaning more into her mother's hug.

"Well, it's way too early in the morning for this talk, and I've got to go to work in the morning. Ranch doesn't take care of itself you know." Johnathon replied leaving the room as he pulled the shells from the shot gun and still mumbling under his breath.

"Sorry, Mom. It's just that the dream was so real." Nakoma said, pulling back to look at her mother, tears still streaming down her face.

"No, no, no, my dear, it's okay. We all have bad dreams from time to time." Mary conveyed, pulling tissue from the tissue box on Nakoma's nightstand, and handing it to Nakoma.

"But it was so real, Mom." Nakoma said as she leaned more into her mother's embrace, wiping the tears with the tissue.

"Dreams can do that, my daughter. It's early still, but in the morning, we can talk more over breakfast." Mary replied as she got up and went to the door of the room, turning out the bedroom light. Mary closed the door part way leaving it slightly open. Bob the cat jumped up onto her bed by her pillow, curling up into a ball, and began to purr away.

"Thanks, Bob. I love you too, but you almost got Dad to shoot a hole in the roof." Nakoma lay back down, trying to fall asleep. The massive buck stood outside her window peering through the crack, watching as she fell back to sleep. Nakoma never noticed as she rolled over crinkling her pillow under her head. An old woman appeared next to the buck gazing at her. She glowed with a soft hint of blue and holding a staff. She placed her right hand on the deer's neck, giving him a soft pat.

"It is time, for now she must be ready." The old woman said looking up at the deer. Both then vanished.

CHAPTER 2
THE NEXT MORNING

The next morning came too soon as the sun peered through the bedroom window. Nakoma didn't feel like dragging her butt out of bed as her mother came to the door.

"Nakoma, breakfast is ready, so wash up and come on." Mary said, whipping her hands with a towel.

"Okay, Mom! Ugghhh..." Nakoma replied with a sigh as she began to roll out of bed. She was a little sore from last night's game. Nakoma made her way to the bathroom to wash up. She began to brush her teeth. While looking in the mirror, she noticed a black smudge on her chin. She grabbed her washcloth and rubbed it away, not giving much thought as to where it came from. Once she was done washing up, she made her way to the kitchen where the smell of fresh bacon and eggs filled the air. Mary was still in the final preparations of the meal when Johnathon came in with the morning paper and sat at the table. He began to open the paper up and finish his morning coffee. Mary then swatted the paper with her kitchen towel.

"Not at the table, John!" Mary scolded looking disappointed that he still had not learned after all these years.

Johnathon grumbled and got up with his cup of coffee and newspaper heading back out to the front porch. mumbling the whole way.

"Sorry about last night, Mom!" Nakoma told her mother. Mary turned around and just smiled as she brought Nakoma her plate.

"So, tell me about your dream, dear." Mary asked as she stood in front of Nakoma. Nakoma looked at the plate and smiled. Her mother had made a smiley face out of the two eggs over easy and a strip of bacon. She had always said to start your day with a smile. Mary than grabbed another plate of bacon and placed it in the center of the table.

"It was so real. The deer was magnificent, and I was about to pet him when this bird like creature came in out of nowhere. There was lightning and thunder that knocked me down, and fire and smoke everywhere." Nakoma began to explain as Johnathon came back in.

"The tribal council is having an open forum tonight for the local farmers and the spending plans. I should be there." Johnathon said placing his coffee cup back on the table and folding up the paper on the corner. The paper began to fall as he caught it.

"Any more thought about going to Colorado University Nakoma?" Johnathon asked now looking at her.

"Dad, Colorado is a good university, and, yes, it would be a great place to study, but I do have options of where I get my education." Nakoma replied, grabbing her fork to eat her breakfast.

"I'm just saying everything you want is there, education wise, and we could get season tickets to the games, so we could come see you at the campus." Johnathon said folding up the newspaper some more and placing it back on the table.

"I know Dad. It would give you a good reason to come see the all American Jeromia Red Cloud. I play a sport too you know!" Nakoma said sarcastically as she continued to eat her breakfast.

"Lacrosse is not a real sport, Nakoma. It is like women's field hockey. It is not a professional sport." Johnathon said, giving her a crinkled face expression back at her.

"Johnathon Standing Elk!" Mary exclaimed, smacking him again with the towel.

"Then why do I have a scholarship to Colorado to play then? That is if I decide to go to Colorado. I just might go to Utah State!" Nakoma said sarcastically, taking a bite out of a piece of bacon. Her face giving him a look of what else can you say.

"Wherever you decide to go to school at, Nakoma, we will support your decision. Isn't that right John?" Mary said poking Johnathon in the ribs with the handle of the spatula.

"Um... Yes, we will be behind you one hundred percent." As John rubbed his side. Nakoma's phone buzzes with a text.

"Oh, it's Debbie, she's on her way to pick me up. I got to get ready. UCLA I might just go there!" Nakoma finished the rest of her breakfast and ran her plate to the sink and rinsed it off.

"Where are you going? I thought you had work today!" Her father said, looking upset and disappointed.

"Nope, took the weekend off to go to Colorado University with Debbie. There is this Native American exhibit this weekend, that I really want to see, and someone must keep Debbie out of trouble. On the plus side, I can see the campus without hearing about your all American." Nakoma said sarcastically as she ran to her room with Bob the cat close behind.

"He's the first Native American- all American to play for a major college!" Johnathon shouted as she left the room. Her mother shot him a look of disappointment, swatting him again with the towel.

"I'm going to the field. At least the cows won't judge me!" As he got up from the table ready to head out the door.

"Uh-huh...Johnathon Standing Elk, you're forgetting something." Mary told him as he turned back around to put his plate away and gave her a kiss on the cheek before leaving.

"Thank you, love you, too, you're welcome for breakfast, you stubborn old mule." Mary replied feeling that she was not appreciated by him or that she mattered.

Johnathon and Mary Standing Elk have been married for close to 20 years. It was a full-time job being rancher. Most years it was good, though they had seen their fair share of hard times as well. With fences falling down and cattle running off, veterinarian bills, or equipment breaking down. It was hard work, but Johnathon loved it. Mary took care of the house and garden. Most of all making sure Nakoma's needs were met. Johnathon's main worry was how much college was going to cost him. He did not have the heart to tell Nakoma that he couldn't pay for it. He could not understand that she already had three full ride scholarships. So as her senior year has drawn to it's end, his anger and frustration had grown. All in all, he did care and wanted her to succeed. Mary on the other hand always looked like she had it together, but she knew her baby girl was becoming a woman.

A half hour later Debbie was honking her cars horn down the driveway. Debbie was driving a pink convertible Volkswagen Bug with those silly aftermarket eye lashes on the head lights. Debbie Lawson was a five-foot two skinny twig who might have weighed a hundred pounds soaking wet. She was cute and she wore more make up than should be allowed by any one person, but she was Nakoma's best friend since elementary school. Over the last school year has totally gone boy crazy. Nakoma loved her like a sister, so she felt compelled to keep her out of trouble.

Debbie pulled up to the house, honking her horn and yelling for Nakoma to come on. The radio was playing loud as she sat up on the seat blowing bubbles with her bubble gum. Nakoma's mom came to the door holding it open with a disappointed look on her face.

"I know your parents raised you better than that, Debbie Lawson. Now get in here and act right." Mary scolded, as Debbie turned the car off.

"Yes, ma'am!" Debbie responded as she got out of the car and ran to the house.

"Where are your shoes, young lady?" Mary said as Debbie ran by. She closed the door. Shaking her head.

Nakoma was in her room still getting ready as Debbie came crashing, in landing on the bed. Bob bolted from the bed and ran out the room. Nakoma was still brushing her hair as she turned and laughed at Debbie's entrance.

"Come on, girl, what's the hold up?" Debbie asked as she blew another bubble with her gum and trying to pull her really tight shorts down a little.

"Come put this in my hair." Nakoma asked as Debbie got off the bed and took the leather hair tie from Nakoma.

"When you gonna cut this big horse mane any ways? It is already past your ass. It's summertime and it's way too hot for all this." Debbie continued to wrap the strap in her hair.

"Before our senior year ends. I'm giving it to the kids with cancer at St. Jude." Nakoma said as she smiled in the mirror. It always made her feel good to do that for the younger kids that struggled with just trying to be normal.

"They probably gonna get ten wigs out of this. Damn, girl." Debbie replied as she finished putting the strap in her hair and could not help but know it was for good cause.

"Let's get a move on I've been dreaming of this day all week, shit, all year!" Debbie said.

"I know that's right!" Nakoma said sarcastically as she put on some earrings and a necklace, finishing it off with a dab of perfume behind each ear.

"Football team... boys... chest all bare, muscles flexing, mmm, mmm, mmm." Debbie was feeling herself up, closing her eyes and smiling.

"Yeah, yeah." Nakoma said as she grabbed her blue jean jacket and her overnight bag.

"We are going to see the college and the art exhibit. Not boys!" She said with a mothering look to Debbie.

"Most of all, I have to keep you out of trouble." Nakoma said as she made it to the bedroom door and turned back to Debbie.

"Can't. That's my middle name." Debbie replied smiling like an innocent child and blowing another bubble of her gum.

"Yeah, I know. let's go." Nakoma and Debbie left the bedroom, making their way to the kitchen. Mary was busy cutting potatoes, and Bob the cat jumped on to the kitchen table.

"No, Bob, get down from there." Mary said as she shooed him with the towel. Bob scrambled back to the floor, running back to Nakoma's room.

"Bye, Mom!" Nakoma gave her mother a hug and kiss on the cheek.

"Hold on. Sunday before midnight, you hear? got your cell, money?" Mary asked checking to make sure she was prepared for her trip.

"Yes, Mama, bye, Mama." Nakoma said as she headed for the door.

"Bye, Mrs. Standing Elk!" Debbie said, giving her a hug as well and then running to door behind Nakoma. Mary just shook her head at the two.

The girls ran to the car and hopped in, tearing out the driveway toward Colorado University. The drive was about a six and half hours to the campus. At first, Debbie could not do anything but talk about the football players who would be on campus. The team's preparation time for next season was already under way. That meant that the whole team would be there, and Debbie would be like a kid in a toy store. After about 45 minutes of Debbie's jabbering, Nakoma turned the radio up, and began singing along to the newest Jonas Brothers song, and Debbie followed suit.

The girls made a quick stop in Johnsonville for fuel and snacks. It would be another two and half hours later when the girls arrived at the campus, they found a parking spot by an old oak tree. The girls made their way to an information stand and picked up a campus map. Nakoma made marks on the map where she wanted to go and what she wanted to see. There were people everywhere, professors carrying their class work, parents helping their kids settle in, and students lounging around in the grass areas soaking in the sun. There were students protesting, others signing up for clubs, activist of all kinds, and most of all Debbie's favorite, boys! Nakoma had to admit one thing is that there would be a lot of distraction coming to a major University like this. She also had to admit Debbie is right. There are a lot of cute guys here. She also knew leaving her small town for the first time made her home sick. The farm is all she has ever known. With this trip she would see if she had what it takes to be on her own.

CHAPTER 3

MY FATHER

The day before-
"Back to you, Gale!"

"Thanks, Dan. Samuel Red Cloud is the chief of the Sioux Nation and has done an impeccable job leading the Native American people into the modern times of today. Not only has he brought countless jobs to the reservations, but he has been a front runner and a fighting force defending all Indian nations' heritage, cultures, and beliefs. Earlier today Chief Red Cloud gave opening introductions at Colorado University's Grant Hall, where artifacts, art, and timeless relics will be on display for the weekend. This display is for everyone to come see and share in the rice culture. There are hundreds of pieces from all across the United States and from many different tribes, taking you thousands of years of history back in time. Here's a clip from the opening introductions."

"Good morning ladies and gentlemen. I am Samuel Red Cloud. I bring to you today many pieces of Indian history for your viewing. It is a display of our Native cultures and heritage from across these United States. Let us not

forget to give thanks to Colorado University for allowing us to be here, and I hope that you can take a glimpse of-"

"Well, we seem to be having technical difficulties with the video. We apologize for the inconvenience. But these rare pieces will be on display all weekend at the university. Now to Chuck for your local sports update."

Samuel Red Cloud threw his whiskey glass at the TV, shattering the glass and TV into a broken black screen. Samuel stood in total anger.

"Arghh…" Samuel said as his son, Jeromia, sat on the couch, now nervous because of his father's anger. The bodyguards George and Lou looked up from the table in the dining area at the confusion.

"Come on, Father, it was good." Jeromia said, shifting to a more defensive posture on the couch, ready for his father to strike him.

"Shut it, boy. They made a fluff piece out of it." Samuel growled, still enraged by the whole thing. Then he was making his way to the drink bar.

"I'm just saying." Jeromia said as he sat up on the couch. Then Samuel came over to his son and backhanded him onto the floor.

"I said shut your mouth and wake up, Jeromia. The white man will never see us for who we are or what we can become. Why do you think I have pushed you all these years to be the best, constantly teaching you and show- ing you how to be the strongest physically and mentally? I have given you the tools and you have become an all- American in their eyes. You are the first Native American to become an all-American hero to your people. A guiding light of hope of what we can become." Samuel said as he finally made his way back to the drink bar to fix himself another glass of scotch. There was a knock at the door, and Samuel nodded in approval to George that it was okay to let them in. An elderly man came into the room holding a small crate.

"I have brought what you requested Chief Red Cloud." The old man said quacking from the weight of the crate.

"Good, good, come set it there on the table." Samuel replied putting the cap back on the scotch bottle and making his way towards the old man.

"Chief it is not wise to toy with the great spirits." The old man said, backing away from the table after putting the crate down.

"That will be all, now leave." Samuel motioned with his hand as to shew the old man away, paying no heed to the old man's warning. The old man left the room and Samuel took a drink of his scotch standing at the table looking at the crate.

"What is it father?" As Jeromia got up and walked over to the table with his father. Rubbing his face from the new shiner he got.

"I've pushed you son, so you would be the best, and you have made me proud. But you also know my passion in the knowledge and power of our native spirit world. The myths, and legends are not just stories there real and I have seen some of them in my life on this earth. I seek the capabilities to tap into what some might say is god like power." Samuel took another drink of his scotch and then placed the glass on the table. Then he pulled out a pocketknife. Samuel looked at his two guards George and Lou by the door.

"Take ten boys!" He told them, and they proceeded out of the room. Samuel then carefully opened the crate with his knife. He began to pull the packing materials away till he could see what was there.

"What is it father?" Jeromia eagerly looking into the crate, not to obstruct his father's view.

"This- if I'm right my son- this is the one thing that can bring back the fabled Thunderbird. The Native cultures have told stories for centuries of a mighty bird that could rain down thunder and lightning, destroying all who cross it's path." Samuel placed his hands on the relic and held it up to inspect it closer.

It was a harness that would be worn around the shoulders of the chosen warrior. It was in perfect condition, as though it had never aged a day. Beads were sewn into the leather in the shapes of two lightning bolts on either side. Feathers surround the bottom edges of the harness, and in the center a stone, or crystal you might say.

"It is said that the leather of the harness was taken for the first chiefs' horse. A mustang! Forged by the first shamans to contain the spirit of the Thunderbird. Warriors from the tribes would compete everyone hundred years to become the next Thunderbird." Samuel put the harness down and picked up his glass to take a drink.

"Spirits, gods, this ain't the movies father." Jeromia said looking at his father like he just went off the deep end.

"No, it is not son, now go do college stuff, make friends." Samuel told his son then took another drink of his scotch.

Jeromia left his father's penthouse suite at the Grand Hotel and headed back to campus in his Porsche 911. It was clean, black, and trimmed in gold right down to the rims. The license plate read (NATVSON). As Jeromia arrived back at the college dorm, his roommate David was sitting on the front steps smiling when he saw the Porsche pull in. Jeromia was parking his car as David ran over to him.

"Hey David. How is it going?" Jeromia replied as he was getting out of the car.

"Dude, where have you been? There are parties lined up in every corner of this campus. Tonight, is going to be epic." David replied, holding a football in his hands, hoping around with excitement.

David Volinski is a second year Full Back for the University, He is five ten and two hundred and fifteen pounds, a total party hound, and most of all Jeromia's roommate. The only thing he likes more than football is girls.

"I was with my father." Jeromia said as he continued to walk to the dorm.

"He's kind of dick if you ask me." David replied, as Jeromia turned around and punched him in the chest hard. David groaned with a gasp for air dropping the football and clutching his chest.

"He's my father, a great man, and you will not call him that to my face." Jeromia said, standing in front of David ready to punch him again.

"Dude, Sorry. I'm sorry, okay? Where did you get that shiner?" David said as he cocked his head to one side looking at Jeromia's face.

"Leave it alone David." Jeromia replied turning back toward the dorm.

"Okay, Okay, let's go get ready." David said picking up the football and rubbing his chest as he walked behind Jeromia.

That evening the two young men made their way to the Delta Phi frat house where you could hear the music for at least a mile away. Several members of the Universities football team were already there. It looked like a scene out of Animal House.

Guys and girls already passed out on the front lawn. Toilet paper stung across the trees and shrubs of the house. It was not long before Jeromia was drunk as well. For someone who was six foot two and two hundred and forty pounds, he could not hold his liqueur.

David called for a cab to take him back to the dorm. Once the cab arrived, David helped Jeromia into the cab and told the cab driver to take him back to the dorm. On the way Jeromia came to long enough once on the road to tell the cab driver to take him to the Grand Hotel.

Once he arrived at the hotel, Jeromia paid the driver, and made his way to his father's penthouse suit front door, where his father's armed guards George and Lou awaited. The two guards George and Lou looked like to overgrown hulks. Looking more the team's offensive line, as they came toward Jeromia. He stumbled forward as they detained him. They grabbed him under each arm to hold him up.

"It's okay, boys, just going to have a chat with my father." Jeromia told them trying not to slur his speech. He continued stumbled as George and Lou effortlessly held him up.

"Hey, I'm alright. Father, Father!" Jeromia began to scream for his father, as George and Lou carried him through the door.

Samuel came into the room tying on a silk red robe, and Jeromia could see just enough into the bedroom that there was a young female lying in his father's bed. Samuel motioned to the guards that it was okay to let his son go. George and Lou let go as Jeromia jerked his body away from them.

"Let me go. Father!" Jeromia stepped away from the two guards and stumbled over to the dining table were the crate still sat. Samuel went to the drink bar to make himself a scotch.

"Son, you're drunk!" Samuel stated to his son, while pouring the scotch into a glass.

"Yes, Father, I'm drunk, and I want to talk." Jeromia braced himself against one of the chairs at the table.

"You never cared about me or Mom. You beat me, tortured me, abuse- me. for what? Did it make you feel better? Was I an interference in your life's work? You care more about these damn relics than you ever have-me!" Jeromia picked up the harness out of the crate.

"Son, put that down. Put down the harness, son!" Samuel began to walk toward his son.

"Oh! This harness, Father?" Jeromia then pulled the harness over his head on to his shoulders. A huge flash of lightning struck the room. Samuel, George, and Lou were thrown into the near-by walls behind them. Jeromia was gone, and there was now a huge whole in the ceiling of the penthouse where he had stood. Lights were flickering, and smoke and water sprayed from pipes above. They looked shocked at what just happened. Crying came from the bedroom, as the young woman covered herself with the sheets.

Samuel got up as the hotels fire alarms began to off. George and Lou just kind of looked at one another for a second in disbelief.

"Get your things and leave now." Samuel said to the young woman. "Lou take her home, and George make the call that we are a go for the operation." Samuel ordered as he went back into the bedroom and got dressed.

Several hours later the building was safe to go back into. Fire fighters had made sure there were no fires or gas leaks. Police detective Lane was on scene checking with staff at the moment asking questions of what happened. Eventually he was directed to Samuel. Samuel had made sure that Lou took care of the nights loose end while George was busy erasing evidence in the bedroom of the chief's companion. He knew the detective would come to him. He also knew that he was protected by officials in high places. Kind of a get out of jail free card you might say.

"Samuel Red Cloud? Evening, I am detective Lane with the police department. Can you tell me what happened tonight?" Lane asked looking at Samuel, and then to the two exceptionally large men with him.

"Maybe in the morning, I will be staying in another room here tonight, so don't worry detective I'm not going anywhere. Here is my card and I am in room 1014 for the evening." Samuel said standing there like he owned the place.

Lane knew of him and his reputation. So, it was against his better judgment, but he knew it would only get dragged out for days if he forced the issue.

"Okay, and here is my card. I will contact you tomorrow morning, and maybe it will help you in trying to tell me from your point of view what happened here tonight." Lane said to him, letting him know that he was not intimidated by him in the least.

Samuel and his two guards made their way back into the hotel for the evening. Detective Lane made sure that there was a uniformed officer for the rest of the night posted near the penthouse suite till he would arrive the next day. Throughout the rest of the evening news reporters would come by asking questions and or film for their news channels of the incident. Only that they were left with that something happened.

CHAPTER 4
MR. FOOTBALL

he next morning, Jeromia's roommate, David came stumbling into their room. He had been out all-night partying. Jeromia was fast asleep on his bed with no shirt on and a torn pair of shorts.

"Hey there, light weight. Oh! What is this? Hey, dude, where did you get the tattoo at, bro? It's sick!" David stumbled his way over to Jeromia's bed to get a closer look.

"Go away, David." Jeromia tried to get comfortable again in his bed.

"No, dude, where did you get the tat?" David took a closer look, and there were no apparent signs of it being fresh.

"I didn't get no new tattoo. My father would kill me." Jeromia rolled over to his back, looking at David to see just how drunk he was.

"Then what's this?" David reached over and touched the tattoo where it looked like a stone in the center of his chest. There was a flash of lightning as David was struck and thrown across the room onto his own bed. Both the young men scrambled to their knees on their beds in total shock of what just happened.

"Ouch, man, that hurt. Not cool, not cool at all." David was grabbing his hand in pain.

"What the hell? Where did this come from?" Jeromia was in total panic mode as fear crossed his face.

"I don't know, man. I just got back, and I see you with this new tattoo." David said grimacing, still clutching his hand in pain.

"It looks just like this old relic my father got yesterday at his penthouse suite. Where is my phone?" Jeromia was now frantically looking for his cell phone. "Help me look for my phone."

"Dude, back pocket." David pointed with the hand that was not hurt.

Jeromia reached into his back pocket and pulled his cell phone out. The phone was completely burnt and would not power up. It was destroyed to say the least.

"Let me see your phone, David." Jeromia motioned for David to throw him his phone. David tossed him the phone, and he began to call his father. "Father, are you okay?"

"Jeromia, are you okay, son? Where are you?" Samuel asked actually conveying concern in his tone.

"I'm fine Father, but I have this tattoo of the harness you got yesterday, and I'm freaking out, David touched it and it blew him across the room, with a bolt of lightning What's going on Father?" Jeromia sat on the edge of his bed, head down looking at the floor.

"Calm down, son. I'm fine, and I will be coming to get you soon." Samuel hung up his phone as he turned back toward the police detective. "Detective Lane, my apologies. Where were we?"

"Everything all right with your son, Mr. Red Cloud?" Samuel nodded to the detective, affirming to him it was okay to continue with his questioning.

"So, you're saying you have no idea of what happened last night."

"No, I do not. Maybe it was a bomb, or a gas leak. I was asleep when I heard the explosion, detective." Samuel motioned for his guards to come to him.

"George go get the car, and Lou call my contractor to fix the hotel." Samuel continued to put his suit coat on as the detective looked at him in frustration.

"I can't let you leave yet." Detective Lane said firmly.

"Detective Lane, I cannot begin to try to explain what happened here. I was asleep in my room alone. But I will say this, a man in my position can make a lot of enemies, and I do make a lot of enemies. I am the victim here, and if you have any more questions contact my attorney."

Samuel turned to the front door of the room and proceeded to walk out. Detective Lane stood there and watched him leave. Lane had no probable cause to detain him, but he knew he was involved.

Jeromia sat there on the edge of his bed with his face planted into the palms of his hands. Trying to remember last night's events.

"Dude, is he okay? What happened over there?" David asked, still shaken up about getting blasted across the room.

"Yeah, He's fine. He didn't tell me what happened, only thing was that he was coming to get me." Jeromia sat there running his fingers through his hair.

"Dude, let's go grab a bite to eat at the cafeteria and then go check the new hotties coming in this next year." David said jumping out of his bed acting like he was shaking it all off.

Dave always seemed to have a knack for getting someone to smile or laugh regardless of what ever funk they were in. It was the first time in Jeromia's life he was truly scared. His father would tell him to man up, and he was right. Jeromia thought to himself. He got up from his bed and changing clothes. He had totally tuned David out.

"Dude, Hello Mr. Football, you listening to me? Hello!" Dave said as he threw a dirty sock at Jeromia.

"Hey, yeah, I hear you. Let's go get something to eat. Last one there is buying." Jeromia bolted out the door, David giving close chase behind.

Later that afternoon, the two young men were throwing the football around in front of the campus entrance grass area. David was having too much fun checking out every girl who walked by. His hand was feeling better as well.

"Dude, come on, look around you. They're everywhere. It's like they're falling from the sky." David said, smiling and winking at girls.

"Yeah, they are, right out of the sky..." That was when Jeromia saw her for the first time. He stopped right in his tracks. Time just stood still in that moment as Nakoma, and Debbie made their way down the sidewalk looking at a campus map. David noticed the expression on Jeromia's face, seeing his eyes were locked on the two girls.

"Dude, go long." David snatched the ball from Jeromia's hands and threw the ball. Jeromia suddenly snapped out of his trance he was in and ran for the pass toward the two girls. Jeromia quickly realized what had just happened and slowed his pace. The ball landed in front of Nakoma's feet, causing the girls to stop. Jeromia made his way over to the girls.

"Sorry, ladies, my friend David has a problem. We don't let him out much." Jeromia said as he couldn't help but look into Nakoma's eyes.

"That's okay Mr. Football. We'll forgive him this time." Nakoma replied picking up the football and tossing it to Jeromia.

"Huh! Mr. Football. So, you've heard of me?" Jeromia said, still looking into her eyes.

"You and how you're going to help Colorado University win a national championship are all my father has talked about this year. So, yes, I've heard of you Jeromia Red Cloud." She placed her left hand on her hip in a sarcastic manner, trying cover her nervousness from his stare. David came jogging on over with a big smile on his face, looking Debbie up and down.

"Ladies, I'm David, and you already met our all American. Did he mention that there is a party in the quad tonight?" David was loving the fact he was holding a conversation with girls.

"No, he did not, cutie. What time will you be there?" Debbie said, moving closer to David returning the look back to him like he was a treat.

"We are not staying that long here on campus, so no thanks." Nakoma said, looking at Debbie like she lost her mind. Debbie looked back at her as if saying how dare you.

"So, what's your major going to be?" Jeromia said, trying to get Nakoma's eyes on him one more time.

"History with a minor in science." Nakoma replied. She liked the way he looked at her.

"Okay, you should meet my father." Jeromia said with a smile, trying to get her to smile back.

"I know who your father is- Samuel Red Cloud, chief of the Sioux Nation, avid archaeologist and obtainer of rare artifacts. That is why we are here today, to see the exhibit." Nakoma ran her fingers through her hair. A long black limousine pulled up in the parking lot right front of them.

"That would be my father. Would you like me to introduce you?" Jeromia said kind of giving a smirk that Nakoma did find cute.

"That's okay. We have to be going."

After watching Jeromia walk towards the car. Jeromia then turned tossing the ball to David. David was busy exchanging numbers with Debbie, as he fumbled to catch the ball.

"It was nice meeting you..." Jeromia said with a pause, trying to see if Nakoma would tell him her name.

"Oh! Nakoma. It was nice to meet you too." Nakoma said with a smile.

"Nakoma!" Jeromia smiled as he said her name, and the look that Nakoma gave him said she liked the way he said it. "It was nice to meet you Nakoma." Jeromia then turned and got into the limousine and drove away.

CHAPTER 5

CHOSEN

Jeromia sat next to his father in the limousine.

"Where is the harness?" Samuel asked looking right at him.

"I don't have it. I got drunk at a party and got into a cab. This morning, I was in my bed at the dorm. I woke up with this tattoo of the harness." Jeromia pulled off his T-shirt to show his father.

"Interesting!" Samuel said, reaching out to touch the tattoo. Jeromia pulled away for he knew what it did to David.

"You came to the penthouse last night drunk. You were raving of how I was such a bad father. In your anger toward me, you picked up the harness and put it on. There was this explosion, and you were gone. I was not hurt, fortunately. Where you stood there is a large hole in the penthouse roof." Samuel said as he inspected the tattoo closer.

"All I know is I woke up with this tattoo and, when David touched it, he was blasted across the room by a lightning bolt."

Jeromia was starting to show a great deal of stress as he put his T-shirt back on.

"Well, I believe that your new tattoo there, son, is the harness. I also believe that you have been chosen to be the Thunderbird of legend." Samuel began to pour himself a glass of scotch from the small bar in the limo.

"You mean this thing has turned me into a monster?" Jeromia said, now running his figures through his hair. His eyes were opened so wide in total horror.

"No, no, no, not a monster, into a god! One of the most powerful gods of our culture. We just have to find out how to control it." Samuel said, taking a drink of his scotch.

"No, I don't want it! I wanna play football and enjoy college." Jeromia said, now getting more upset at the idea of his new life.

"Who says you can't do both? It is up to you to try, but you have been chosen to do one." Samuel said, picking up the USA Today. Jeromia, now with his hands pressed against his forehead, bent over in the seat, crying, "No, no, no." Samuel tossed the paper to his son, with an article face up to him.

"I think you were in Kansas last night after your meeting with me." Jeromia looked at the paper that read, Wildfires Sweep across Kansas Wheat Fields. "I made some phone calls about the area. Found out the local farmers signed a deal with the federal government to run oil pipelines right up into Cheyenne territories. There has been no discussion with tribal leaders in the area. The American government continues to take from all of us. They voted it in without our voice being heard."

31

Samuel took another drink. "You are chosen to wear the mantle, and bring justice to our people, our lands."

Samuel took another drink, as the limousine pulls up to Jeromia's dorm. Jeromia exited the vehicle, still appearing to be in shock of the whole thing.

"Get a new phone and live your college dream. I'll contact you if I discover anything of interest." Samuel said as Jeromia closed the door to the limousine.

"Yeah, right, live the college dream." Jeromia said under his breath, walking away. When he made it back to his dorm where he crashed till that evening.

Nakoma and Debbie made their way to Grant Hall for the exhibit. There were thousands of artifacts. Some were almost three thousand years old. They were from all over the United States. Nakoma was like a kid in a candy store. Debbie, on the other hand, was trying to find a cute guy to talk to. The girls made their way to what appeared to be the east wing to the hall. As the girls entered, there was only one pedestal in the center of the room where a little old lady was busy using a feather duster. On the pedestal was a beautiful Native headdress. Nakoma turned to tap Debbie on the shoulder, but her friend was skipping off to go talk to a security guard at the doorway. As Nakoma turned back to the head dress, the little old lady cut in front of her, continuing to act like she was dusting around the headdress. Nakoma moved to the left of the lady where she could see the headdress better. It was a beautiful gold band with an eagle, bear, elk, fish, and a snake. There was a stone on the left side that looked like a mix between a diamond and a turquoise stone, and there were five eagle feathers fixed to the back of that.

As she got within a few feet of the headdress it began to glow like the aurora borealis. Just then, the little old lady cut in front of Nakoma, still acting like she was dusting.

"Hey, I'm standing here, rude lady." She said as the little old lady turned around and dusted her face with the duster. She looked at her like she was totally a crazy old woman. The old lady turned back around as if she were still cleaning. Debbie came running back into the room.

"Excuse me, Ma'am? Ma'am, this piece does not have a placard on it. Do you know what tribe it's from or how old it is?" Nakoma asked as the little old lady who continued dusting.

"Hey, girl, the security guard, Michael there, is going to give me the grand tour." Debbie said, just then Debbie's phone rang.

"Tell David I said hello." The little old lady said to Debbie, giving Nakoma a wink and a smile.

Debbie looked at the old lady and then at her phone. She was right. It was David calling. She answered her phone and walked back out of the room. Nakoma's curiosity was piqued now.

"How did you know that was David? Why is this headdress glowing like that? And who are you?" Nakoma asked the old woman.

"Lucky guess, I guess. It calls to you, and I'm GES!" The lady replied.

"Calls to me... What are you saying? Like it wants me or needs me or that it's mine by some weird chosen path?"

"Sort of, in a way that all before you have been chosen to wear it. Now it calls to you." GES said as she began to

33

walk around behind Nakoma. Nakoma could not take her eyes off the headdress. She was mesmerized by it's glow.

"Go ahead. Put it on. You cannot deny it's call now." GES said, as to now she was behind Nakoma.

Nakoma turned around to look at her, and the lady was gone. She began to look around the room. No one else was there. She could see Debbie talking to the security guard outside the room. As she turned back around, she could now hear voices calling to her. It was almost like Nakoma was in a trance. She picked up the head dress and put it on. Instantly, she was flashing through a tunnel of many colors till she came to a dark area. She could feel that her feet were on a solid surface but could not see anything. A fog came in around her, giving off some sort of blue hue. Just then, she could hear someone coming towards her. As the person got close, it sounded like they tapped a staff on the ground. Light filled the room, as Nakoma looked now right at GES holding a staff that was giving off a blue light.

"Now, where were we? Oh yes, you have been chosen, Spirit Walker. The world we live in has been overrun with hate. The evil spirits have returned, and it is your job to keep the balance." GES said as she approached Nakoma.

"Chosen... Spirit Walker... Where are we? This is not the east wing of Grant Hall." Nakoma said, still looking around at the blue fog that seemed to be all around her.

"No, no, it is not, but there never was an east wing to Grant Hall. My apologies, deary, Introductions, yes!" As if she were speaking to more than just Nakoma.

"I am the Great Elder Spirit, but you can call me GES for short."

"So where are we?" Nakoma replied, and GES could tell that Nakoma showed no real signs of fear of her surroundings, relaxing in her posture.

"The spirit world. This is where you will come train and get advice from the elder spirits." GES said, smiling to see Nakoma finally focusing on her.

"Why am I the chosen one or Spirit Walker?" Nakoma asked, now focusing on GES's illuminated staff.

"I've watched you from a very young age, Spirit Walker. Through the years, I could see the gift in you growing. Ask yourself this: Why is it that animals seem to be drawn to you as if they are a family pet like Bob? You are energetic in learning history, and you feel naturally attuned to helping others. Your friend Debbie is a slut, but you feel the urge to protect her." GES said, taking her hand off the staff. It continued to stand up all on it's own.

"How do you know all these things, and what are these other voices I hear?" Nakoma said, looking at the blue fog around her.

"Like I said, I know everything about you, Spirit Walker, and the voices you hear are the elder spirits. In time, you will learn to commune with them, growing in your new powers and knowledge to aid you in your journey." GES, at this point, had now walked all the way around Nakoma and was back holding her staff.

"How do I get out of here?" She replied, and GES just smiled back at her.

"The answer to that, Spirit Walker, Is where do you want to be?" GES said, tapping her staff on the floor and was gone taking the light with her.

"I wanna be with my friend Debbie!" Nakoma said, now standing in the dark with the blue fog all around.

"Can anyone give me some light." She asked as the blue fog became brighter, illuminating the area around her.

CHAPTER 6

NEW POWERS

Nakoma now focused on the area she was in. It was like a deep cavernous cave. She could hear a waterfall in the distance and seeing trees that were all lit with the same blue hues. The fog that she once was seeing now seemed more like a little sphere with a blue smoke trails. They scattered into the whole area when she asked for more light. They moved all around slowly, like a piece of lint drifting in a soft breeze. She could hear voices as they passed by.

"These must be the great spirits." She said, seeing millions of lights looking throughout the cavern. She had to think of way out of there. No matter how much she thought of her friend, nothing happened. She clapped her hands. She clicked her heels together three times. But there seemed to be no way back to her friend.

Then she thought about her bed in her home. Just like that, she was lying in her bed in her bedroom. She jumped to her feet, looking around her room. She was really there, as she looked at the things in her room. She saw the newspaper article and photo of her high school championship that the team just won. Then she looked at the mirror on her door. She was wearing a hide dress that went over her left shoulder with slits up both sides. It hugged her body well and still gave full range of movement. Her boots were of thick leather with fur at the top and straps along the outside. She had two leather bracers with brass plating along them and fur at both ends. There were armbands on each her upper arms with a turquoise stone in the center and each had two quail feathers. Around her neck was a traditional bone choker with another turquoise stone.

"Spirit Walker, more like warrior princess!" She said as she checked herself out in the mirror.

"*All that's missing now is a bow and arrows*." She thought, and just like that, a bow appeared in her left hand and arrows on her back strapped over the right shoulder. She began to smile, then she heard her mother coming. Nakoma began to panic, and then she thought of Debbie's car.

She was now sitting in Debbie's car, looking around to see if anyone else saw her appear. Lucky for her, no one was even in the area. Nakoma took the headdress off, and she was instantly back in her regular clothes. She stared at it, wondering where she could put it.

"It would be easier if you were a bracelet." She said, and just like that the headdress became a bracelet. "Okay!"

She placed the bracelet on her left wrist and took another look around to see if the coast was clear. She got out of the car and made her way back to the exhibit. As Nakoma arrived, she heard a woman on the loudspeaker.

"We will be closing the exhibit in fifteen minutes. Thank you for coming, and we hope to see you again for future shows."

"That's impossible the exhibit doesn't close till 5:00 p.m." She looked at her phone. It was a quarter till five.

"I've lost almost three hours with this thing." She looked at the bracelet.

"There you are! I've been looking for you everywhere." Debbie said as she approached, holding the arm of a security guard. "Oh! This is Michael, and he has been such a peach helping me look for you."

"Debbie, we have to go. We need to talk right now." Nakoma said with a look of urgency on her face.

"Okay. Later, sugar, and thank you again for your big strong help." She turned back to blow Michael a kiss good-bye. Michael just smiled, grabbing the front of his security belt like he was the man. The girls made their way back to the parking lot as Nakoma was tried to explain her story of all that just happened to her.

"Girl, you are tripping." She looked at Nakoma with a what kind of drugs are you on look.

"No, I'm serious. Look at this bracelet. It's the head-dress from the exhibit." Nakoma removed the bracelet and imagined it as the headdress. Debbie watched as the bracelet instantly became the head dress. She jumped back in shock thinking some weird magic trick had just been played on her.

"Wow, girl, that's like some next level freaky shit there."

"I know, right? As I got closer to it, it began to glow, and I could hear these voices. Then I put it on, and I was then standing in this dark cave with these tiny little lights that had blue smoke trails coming off of them. The lady

39

GES said that I was the chosen one. I am to be the next Spirit Walker." Nakoma then paused, looking at Debbie. Debbie was looking at her like she had just lost her mind.

'What kind of drug have you taken? Did you go to a sweat without me? If so, put it on again." Debbie shot back at Nakoma, not believing a word she just said. Nakoma took a quick look around as they made their way on over to an old oak tree. No one was around that she could see. Nakoma closed her eyes and placed the headdress back on her head. She opened her eyes and saw see was back in the spirit world. GES was standing before her holding the staff that was illuminated.

"Now, where were we, Spirit Walker?" GES said pondering a look into the air.

"You left me here, not telling me how to get out." Nakoma said, stomping her foot.

"Anger is never a good thing. We will have to work on that. Oh, yes, your training Spirit-" GES was cut short.

"Training? How about you tell me how I lost almost three hours today?" In the blink of an eye, Nakoma was slapped in the back of the head by GES as she walked back in front of her.

"Focus, Spirit Walker, there is much to do and learn if you are to combat the evil spirits of this world." GES turned back around to face Nakoma.

"Ouch, you old-" Nakoma was stuck again as GES walked from behind her again.

"Focus, Spirit Walker. Being rude does not suit you." As she walked back in front of her, turning back around again to face Nakoma. Nakoma stood there silent this time, rubbing the back of her head. The look on her face was one of frustration.

"Your powers come from the spirits of this world. From all living things and those from the past. You are connected to everything in this world."

"Like a Jedi Knight from Star Wars?"

"In a sense, yes, but you are connected directly into the spirit of every living thing while you wear the headdress. You can feel their emotions, fear, and love.

"You are my Yoda!" Nakoma said jokingly to her.

"You will learn to use the spirits around you in your fight to stop the evils in this journey. You said you lost three hours. Why do you think that is?"

"Because I thought of other things than where I needed to be! But how do I not do that again?" Nakoma now showed a calmer composure and focus as GES began to smile.

"You are in control of your reality, of the time you spend here or in the world. Your focus is your greatest power or your biggest flaw."

"Without focus, I could lose more than just a few hours-maybe days, or even years." GES nodded to Nakoma, confirming her words. She looked into Nakoma's eyes with intent.

"I've seen it before, and it's a tougher burden to know now that it's important that you learn it quick."

"So, I have to focus on the specific time I left and see myself there. But how do I listen to the voices, and how do I use them to aid me?" Nakoma was now eager to learn more.

"The universe is filled with possibilities. Work hard on your focus and the rest will come. Like I said, you are connected to all things." GES then tapped her staff on the ground and vanished. The area was dark again.

"Spirits of this world, illuminate so I might see."

The area lit up and she could now see. As she looked around, the area got brighter. It was bright like the day but with a beautiful blue huge. There were trees and a huge water fall in the distance. It looked like a gigantic cave. The trees were covered in the lights, and a stream ran through the whole length. Grass and various plants all had a huge of blue to them. Butterflies and fireflies even glowed with the blue. Nakoma began to smile at it's beauty. Though with her saying illuminate, made things brighter. Giving her the opportunity to see more. Then the look on her face became serious.

"I've got to get back to Debbie!" Nakoma began to focus on the time she had left her at the parking lot. In that instant, she was back in front of Debbie.

"Wow! Holy shit, look at you. I mean, Pocahontas, how the hell this happen? Seriously, girl, you need to focus." Debbie stood there looking at Nakoma like she'd just lost her mind.

"What? No, look at me. Can't you see it?" Debbie was looking at Nakoma like she just lost her mind. Nakoma looked at her clothes.

"You need to focus, girl. All I see is that crazy sick bracelet and my best friend losing her mind. Besides, I have the perfect solution, and it's at a party. There's this pool, and boys. Are you sure you're not high on something?"

Nakoma had brought herself back to the point before taking off the bracelet. She was so confused till she looked down at her wrist. She turned away from Debbie. Walked on over to an old oak tree and placed her hand upon the tree.

"*This is real, right? I'm not going crazy, am I?*" She thought to herself, closing her eyes.

"No, you're not crazy Spirit Walker." The voice seemed to come from the tree itself, but it was nurturing and peaceful, giving her comfort. Nakoma opened her eyes, staring at the tree. She could now feel the life in the tree. It's words were as loud as if they had been spoken. She began to cry from the joy that it made her feel.

"Girl, you okay over there?" Debbie made her way over to Nakoma, grabbing her by the arm. "Come on, let's go already." Nakoma wiped the tears from her eyes as she was pulled away from the tree, looking back at it and smiling.

"Focus now. We saw the campus, went to the exhibit, and now it's my turn. We're going to a party because tomorrow we head back home." She continued to drag Nakoma to the car.

"Okay, for a little while, I guess, but we do need to head home tomorrow. As she looked back at the tree, still smiling.

CHAPTER 7
FATES ALIGN

Jeromia lie on his bed tossing the football into the air and catching it. David sat on the edge of his bed, staring at Jeromia.

"Dude lets go get your new phone. Then we can hop on over to the liquor store and grab some brewski's. The party starts at eight. Put some trunks on because there's a pool." David said, trying to get Jeromia out of the funk he was in.

"Yeah, your right, I have to embrace this thing, or it will consume me." Jeromia said, getting up from his bed and tossing the football to David.

"I think that chick Debbie and her friend are going to be there. The things I wanna to do to that ass." David said, closing his eyes, humping the football on his bed, and smacking it as if it were Debbie's ass.

"Nakoma." Jeromia said, staring out his dorm room window with a smile. Then he looked over at David and couldn't help but laugh at him and his depicted version of sex with Debbie.

"Let's go, horndog."

That evening, Jeromia and David were having a good time at the party. The Beta Kappa house was huge in size. There were two DJ's battling it out on the balcony above the pool. There were several kegs of beer throughout the household and backyard. There was a full bar under the balcony and a hot tube. David was in the process of setting up a wet T-shirt contest with several of the girls. Jeromia sat by the pool in a lawn chair babying a beer.

Nakoma and Debbie finished getting a room for the evening just off campus at a local motel called the Bison Inn. Debbie was eighteen already since she had been held back a year by her foster parents in school. Nakoma called for a cab to go to the party. The girls had decided to take the cab based on Debbie's drive to have what she called a "good time." Once they arrived, Debbie jumped out of the cab saying, "Not it!" Nakoma just shook her head and paid the cab driver.

Debbie ran through the house till she found David. "David, there you are!" Debbie said, prancing on over to his side.

"Hey, just in time. We're having a wet T-shirt contest. Would you like to participate?" David said, wrapping his left arm around Debbie's waist.

"I'll pour the water, sugar." Debbie said, grabbing David's left butt cheek, biting her lower lip as she looked him in the eyes. David brought his right fist to his mouth, biting his knuckles, nodding his head in compliance with her offer.

Nakoma entered the frat house, making her way through searching for Debbie. As she came out the back door, she could see Debbie with David. That's when Jeromia saw her. It was the second time that day, and just like before, it was if time slowed down. She made her way past the hot tub and bar, moving right in his direction. Jeromia could see her more clearly than anyone else. His heart began to race as he stood up. He stared upon her face, hoping she would look his way. Nakoma was stopped by some others. They were asking about her hair as Jeromia now made his way towards her. Jeromia took a deep breath. Nakoma looked right at him as he approached. She absently played with her hair, looking into his eyes.

"Hey, you came!" Jeromia said.

"You can thank Debbie for that." Nakoma said, walking past him in the direction of the pool. Jeromia stayed right by her side.

"How was the exhibit?" Jeromia said as he was trying anything to get her to focus on him. It was like now he was dying inside just to see her face.

"Educational, way more than I expected." Nakoma said, finally turning back to face Jeromia, she was fighting it, but the feelings of the passion welled up with every look into his eyes.

"Besides, the exhibit wasn't the only reason I came. The university has a great history program and a good solid science department." Nakoma said, losing composure.

"Well, I'm glad you came." Jeromia said. Just then, the one that they called Bear, a senior defensive nose tackle every bit of 325 pounds, pushed Jeromia into the pool. When Jeromia hit the pool, there was a large explosion of thunder and lightning. Jeromia flew up into the air and hovered about three hundred feet. He looked right at Nakoma. Fear overcame Nakoma as her dream came rushing back. She fell to the ground, scrambling backward to get away as she looked upon the winged creature from her dream. The creature began to scream, lightning filled the skies, and thunder shook the ground. People began to shout and run frantically. Lightning struck the DJ booth, and the speakers and lights began to explode. Nakoma looked for Debbie. She was nowhere to be seen. She got to her knees, taking the bracelet from her wrist and thinking of the head dress. She placed it on her head, and she became the Spirit Walker, looking right at the winged creature.

The creature looked back and flew away. Nakoma thought of the spirit realm, and she was there. She thought of how to track the creature.

"Let me see what he sees." Nakoma said, and instantly she was seeing what the winged creature was seeing. He was flying northwest and fast. Lightning struck through the skies as he flew. His body was part human with huge wings and talons for feet, tail feathers on his backside, and a loin cloth across the front. Within a few minutes, he was in what she could guess might have been Washington state over a logging camp. He began diving toward the logging site. The creature let out a huge scream, sending lightning in a chain striking every piece of equipment there. The thunder broke all the windows of the office trailers. A security guard who had been sleeping in his truck fell out onto the ground in a total terror. The creature began to swoop in on him. Nakoma appeared, putting herself in front of the man. As the creature got closer, Nakoma thought of a copper spear in her hand and stabbed it into the ground. The creature screamed again,

47

sending lightning in their direction, and Nakoma threw up her left arm to block. The lightning struck the spear, causing it to glow red- orange from the heat. Nakoma screamed at the creature. "No!"

The security guard was crying. He had wet himself. The creature landed before her about fifty feet away. The harness on his shoulders glowed like Nakoma's headdress. The stone was emitting an electrical current around it. The creature stood, spreading its wings wide and screaming at Nakoma. Lightning filled the skies, and thunder shook the ground.

"I said no! Leave!" She said sternly. The creature flew up into the air and left. The security guard was now in the fetal position crying for his mother. Nakoma turned around to him, feeling his fear. "He's gone, sir. You're safe!" She said in a ghostly voice.

"He... what was..., who are you?" The guard stammered, scrambling to get away from her.

"I am the Spirit Walker! These lands are Native lands. The company cutting these timbers is doing it illegally and must stop. That is why the Thunderbird attacked. I must leave you now. The logging must stop!" Nakoma said. Her voice was haunting, and her eyes glowed in a blue essence of fiery smoke. The security guard shuddered in fear against the truck. Nakoma disappeared right in front of the guard, going back to the spirit realm.

"Let me see the Thunderbird." Nakoma could now see the creature by a waterfall tucked away in a valley. The creature began to lie down as if to go to sleep. Nakoma appeared before the creature as it began to change back into Jeromia. He was asleep and cold, shivering from the brisk mountain air. Nakoma knelt beside him, touching him on the shoulder. She thought of the motel room. Suddenly she and Jeromia were in the middle of the motel room. Debbie and David jumped as they appeared.

"What the hell! Jeromia, what happened?" David said, grabbing the blanket from the bed to put on Jeromia. David was stark naked. Debbie jumped up, grabbing the sheet to cover herself backing toward the bathroom.

"He has had a long journey tonight and needs rest. Take him back to the dormitory." Nakoma said in her ghostly voice.

"Oh shit, your voice is creepy as hell, and those eyes... yes, back to the dorm, right now, no problem. Debbie, later." David said, trying to pick Jeromia up after putting on his shorts.

"Bye, sweetums. Call me." Debbie said, still staying back from Nakoma.

"Debbie, it's me, Nakoma." She took the headdress off and became her regular self.

"How did you just do that? And that was a badass outfit. But you are really freaking me out right now." She became more at ease sitting back on the bed.

"The old lady at Grant Hall today is actually a Great Elder Spirit. She said I was chosen to be the Spirit Walker." As Nakoma sat on the edge of the bed with Debbie.

"You mean that old decrepit reject from Moana is a great spirit, and you have been chosen to be a warrior princess with a ghost voice and spooky eyes." Debbie said, now more interested in what Nakoma had to say.

"Yes, and don't be rude. I went to this place that's a huge underground cavern with trees lit with these little blue lights that are really elder spirits." Nakoma continued to explain. She continued on for hours as Debbie sat and listened. Finally, the girls fell silent sometime after ten, staring at one another. Within minutes, the two girls fell asleep.

CHAPTER 8

CONTROL

David had managed to flag down a taxi outside the motel. Told the driver to take them to the dorm. It took about 30 minutes for them to arrive. The taxicab pulled up to the football players' dormitory at around ten thirty at night. George and Lou were waiting at the steps dressed in rubber looking suits as David got out of the cab, and he recognized the two men. He had seen them before when Jeromia's dad dropped by.

"Hey, wanna help me out with my buddy here?" David asked as George pushed past him.

"We'll take it from here." Lou said as the two men put on some weird looking gloves and proceeded to take Jeromia out of the cab.

"Um. Please tell Mr. Red Cloud I had nothing to do with this." David said, backing away from the two men.

It was also around eleven at night as Nakoma sat up on her bed in the motel room. She couldn't sleep. Nakoma sat looking at the headdress, wondering if she wanted it at all. Debbie lies on her bed, stirring in her sleep and rambling on how Nakoma ruined a perfect evening. Nakoma then was thinking of how Jeromia came across the power to begin with. She remembered the harness the Thunderbird wore around it's shoulders. The stone in the center closely resembled the stone on her headdress. Maybe Chief Red Cloud found the harness and Jeromia put it on, much like she had done with the headdress. Nakoma now thought of Chief Red Cloud, wondering if he already knew and what that means to her safety. She wondered what it meant to anyone who got in his way.

"Are you listening to me? Hello!" Debbie said, now awake sitting up, ready to throw a pillow at Nakoma.

"Why would you bring David here?" Nakoma said.

'Well, from what I saw. Your all-American blew up the party. Once the police showed up, David and I came here." Debbie was now madder about the fact that her whole weekend was a bust.

"I'm sorry, Debbie! I may have put us into danger. I didn't know you were going to be here." Nakoma said turning the headdress back into the bracelet and putting it on to her left wrist.

"It's going to be fine. David is a goldfish. He'll forget everything by morning. Here, I'll call him now to make sure."

Nakoma began to rub the bracelet in small circles along the stone. Nakoma's eyes turned to a bluish glow.

"Focus. You just got back from the party. You were never in my room. Later, handsome." Nakoma was causing Debbie to say the words to David, transmitting to both in the same trance. A small spell of suggestion of sorts as she used Debbie as the middleman. Not knowing if it would work, but something to her felt like it aided her in doing it.

Then his phone rang. "Hello, miss me already?" David turned back toward his dorm. A strange sound came over the phone. "I was just getting back from the party. Yes, bye beautiful." It was as if David was in a trance as he proceeded up the stairs and into the dorm.

George and Lou took no notice as they put a weird harness on Jeromia's chest area. They also restrained his hands and feet. The cab driver was in shock at what was happening.

"Hey, you can't do that. Who are you guys?" The driver said as he was reached for his cell phone.

"Mr. Red Cloud thanks you for your services, and hopefully this is enough for your trouble." Lou said, handing the driver a hundred dollars.

"Yes, sir, tell Mr. Red Cloud everything is fine here." He carefully took the money from Lou.

Lou and George proceeded to remove Jeromia from the cab. Once they had him removed from the cab, the driver left in a hurry. George pulled vehicle keys from a pocket and unlocked a black panel van that was nearby. The two men placed Jeromia into the back of the van. There were tribal symbols throughout the interior and exterior of the van, looking more like something found in a cave. The men drove away as David looked out his window to watch them leave.

They drove all night till the sun came up the next morning, only stopping for fuel. They arrived at the reservation at around seven in the morning. The two men proceeded through the reservation till they came to the warehouse on the Lakota territory. A heavily armed guard waved them through the gate. As they pulled into the warehouse. Samuel was waiting, leaning on his Porsche 911 and drinking his usual scotch. They removed Jeromia from the rear of the van and took him to the center of the warehouse where there was this glass looking box. But it was a cage in all fairness. It was approximately thirty by thirty feet in diameter. On top of the cage were four Tesla coils in each corner. On top in the center was a rod leading through the roof of the warehouse. The cage was covered in ancient Indian wards. There was a metal platform with three trailers on top, looking more like an observation tower. The trailer facing the cage had windows all the way across. Inside and out there were several people running around in white coats clamoring over equipment. George and Lou moved Jeromia into the cage, and Samuel stood outside observing. Once the two men removed the protective harness, they moved quickly to the door. When the door closed, Jeromia awoke and was freaked out. Lights came on, illuminating the whole area. The light immediately blinded him, causing him to squint.

"What's going on? Father, what are you doing?" Jeromia was now focusing on his father.

"Calm down, son. We are here to help you." Samuel said, moving closer to see his son. "I need you to stay in this room." Samuel gestured to Jeromia's new confinement.

"What are all these symbols for? Are those Tesla coils up there?" Jeromia said, unable to calm down.

"Yes, son, these are here to protect everyone including you." Samuel said.

George and Lou began to put their gloves back on, ready to protect themselves if needed. They feared him and didn't want to get hit again. Samuel knew the cage would hold.

"You're going to imprison me here? What about school? People will notice that I'm gone. Oh god, what did you do to David?" Jeromia knew his father was a ruthless man.

"Son, I need you to do this so we can find out how to remove the harness. Jeromia... You cannot control the harness. It won't be long before you kill someone you shouldn't. So please calm down." Samuel pleaded with Jeromia. Lou and George came to Samuel's side ready to protect him if the cage did not hold. Samuel knew the cage would hold and that George and Lou were being over dramatic with the rubber suits and all.

"You're right, Father, but why all this? I don't want to hurt anyone. Let me go!"

Samuel motioned to a scientist to shoot him with a sedative to knock him back out. The scientist opened a small door hatch on the other side and took a shot at Jeromia with a dart gun. The shot hit him in the back, and Jeromia fell unconscious. Samuel took a deep breath, and George and Lou took off their gloves.

"Thanks, boys! Take care of the roommate. Find out where the taxi driver picked them up at." Samuel said to George and Lou.

"Yes, Mr. Red Cloud." George said as the two men left the warehouse in the van.

"Begin with test one the moment he wakes. Call me when you start." Samuel said as he walked over to his car as well. He drove away quickly as he headed out, leaving rubber in his wake.

CHAPTER 9

FAMILY

he night before-

"How are you so calm with all this? This is some weird ass freaky supernatural shit going on. Chief Red Cloud is not a good man." Nakoma said in frustration.

"You act like he's going to kill us or something." Debbie said as she held up her phone to take a selfie.

"That's what I am saying, Debbie! Since the first casino twelve years ago, there has been an increase in missing persons reports on the reservation. Spirit Rock is full of hope jars for their loved ones. I know it's because of Chief Red Cloud. And now with his son being the Thunderbird... I know he's going to protect it at any cost."

"But you're the Spirit Walker, right? You can stop him." Debbie said with a sarcastic confidence that Nakoma didn't share to be funny. Nakoma just looked at Debbie in disappointment and then with compassion. She now could feel how scared she was. Had Debbie always been scared, and this was just how she dealt with it.

"Okay! Let's go home then." Debbie got up to gather her things. Nakoma followed suite and was beginning to understand how the headdress heightened her senses.

The girls drove the rest of the night, stopping only for gas till they arrived back at Nakoma's farm. As the girls got out of the car, it was in the early morning. They could see the smoke rising up on the non-reservation side. Nakoma's father came driving his pickup in a hurry from the field, coming to an abrupt stop by the barn.

"Nakoma, saddle up. We got to move the herd in case the fire jumps." Her father said, running to the barn.

Nakoma and her father ran to the barn to get the horses ready.

"Debbie, honey, you need to come inside." Nakoma's mother said, holding out her arms to give Debbie a hug. "The roads are shut down, so come on, I'll fix you something to eat." The look on Mary's face said more than she let on.

"Yes, ma'am, I am tired too. I'll call my foster parents after I eat." She said with no real pep in her step, just walking to the house. Mary followed behind.

Nakoma and her father saddled their horses and rode out hard toward the south-east corner of the property, hoping they could get a better look at the fire from the hillside. Once they were there, they could see the blaze coming. The sun was up enough for them to see.

"How did it start Father?" Nakoma asked.

"House fire just across the road from the reservation." Her father said, looking to see which way the wind was blowing.

"Do we know who's house it was?"

"Darnel Cumming's old place." Her father said, still watching the wind.

"That's the meth house two doors down from Debbie's..." Nakoma was now concerned about Debbie's parents.

"We don't know that yet, Nakoma. It has already claimed seven homes and is moving fast onto the res., just hope the winds don't change toward us." Johnathon could see the concern on her face.

"Father, I need to tell you something." Nakoma said, ready to tell him her secret.

"It can wait the winds are shifting this way. Let's get the herd to the north end." Her father said, kicking his horse into a run. Nakoma followed suit.

The two-rode hard and began to drive the herd toward the north field. The bad part of this was that the north field was ready to be cut for the winter hay. They continued to drive the cattle as the winds picked up.

Debbie had her breakfast and then went and lie down on the living room couch. Within a few minutes, she was fast asleep. Mary didn't have the heart to tell her that her home was probably gone. They didn't even know if her parents had made it out okay.

After about an hour of driving the cattle to the north field, they had made it. Nakoma rushed to open the gate as the cattle entered. Once the last heifer was through, she closed the gate behind her.

"Let's get to the pond so the horses can cool off." Her father said, putting his horse into a trot.

"Yes, Father!" Nakoma followed getting back onto her horse.

Firefighting teams were able to control 95 percent of the blaze before it got too far into the reservation.

Nakoma and her father were sitting by the pond when his phone rang.

"Hello. Good news, then. Thank you, Tim!"

Tim Dobbson was a local firefighter, the deputy chief to be exact. He had known their family since he and Nakoma's father were kids. He was Johnathon's best friend and Nakoma's god-father.

"What? Damn meth heads! Sorry, Tim, the girl is at our house now with Mary. I'll tell her."

Just then, there was a large explosion. The two looked back up toward the house as they saw their home go up in pieces. Nakoma and her father jumped to their feet to get onto their horses.

"My house, Tim!" Johnathon dropped the phone, getting on his horse, and he rode hard toward the house with Nakoma close behind. As the two of them approached, they could see a black panel van in the front. Two very large men stood looking at the destroyed home. When the two saw Johnathon and Nakoma riding towards them, they pulled out their guns. Johnathon was now enraged as he saw the two of them. Kicking his horse into a charge, he pulled his knife from his boot, giving a war cry, ready to avenge his wife. The two men began to fire at him. A bullet struck Nakoma's horse, dropping the animal onto Nakoma's left leg. She winced in pain from the weight of the horse. Her father continued the charge as the two men now had better aim as he closed the gap. Johnathon was struck several times as he finally fell from the horse.

"No!" Nakoma cried out as the two men approached his body, reloading their guns. George took aim at Johnathon's head and squeezed the trigger. Johnathon moved no more as Lou made his way toward Nakoma. Nakoma removed the bracelet, turning it into the headdress, and put it on. She vanished right before Lou's eyes.

"GES!" Nakoma screamed as she laid on the ground, clinching her fist and continuing to cry uncontrollably. She still felt the pain of the horse landing on her.

"This is always the hardest part in what I do." GES said standing now in front of Nakoma.

"What do you mean?" Nakoma said, holding her leg that was hurt and breathing heavily.

"Times in this world have changed so much." GES said, as she knelt beside her.

"What do you mean GES?" Nakoma said again. GES touched her leg, and the pain was now gone.

"Simpler times a hundred years ago. No computers! Chief Red Cloud is a very resourceful man. He tracked you and Debbie from the motel records and video surveillance. He has Jeromia, but I cannot see him. He's using spirit wards around him." GES seemed to try to focus on Jeromia.

Nakoma tried to focus on Jeromia. She could not connect with him.

"But I have brought some friends who wanted to see you." GES said, as three spirit lights took form before her. The lights became smoky shapes as they began to form. Then they became her parents and Debbie.

"Mom, Dad, Debbie!" Nakoma rushed to hug her mother but passed right through the smoky shape.

"Focus, Spirit Walker, if you wish to speak with them." GES said, now standing behind her.

Nakoma wiped the tears from her eyes. Her parents and Debbie looked upon her with pride and joy. She stood before them, focusing on each one of them individually.

"You're so beautiful, the dress suits you." Her mother said. Nakoma began to cry even more, wiping tears away as they fell.

"I'm sorry, I'm so sorry" Nakoma continued to cry.

"Don't be, you have made us proud, and I am honored you are my daughter." Her father said, puffing out his chest.

"You're not kidding. This place is amazing, and David is here too. But hey! We're not going anywhere." Debbie said, with a smile.

"We will be with you always from now on. All you have to do is listen." Her mother said, with a smile.

The three of them turned back into the blue spirit orbs, and two of them flew into the bone collar around her neck. A leather string appeared with two beads below the brooch of the collar. Nakoma felt the warm embrace of her parents. She wiped away her tears.

"Oh, one more thing, Spirit Walker. I found him out by the barn." GES said looking behind her as Bob came trotting by.

"Bob!" Nakoma said, dropping back down to her knees, and Bob ran on over to her lap.

"Thank you, GES" Nakoma said, hugging Bob.

"I'll leave you for a while to your thoughts." GES said as she disappeared.

Nakoma sat on the ground holding Bob as he purred in her arms. Blue orbs hovered nearby. She did not know that two days had passed. She stood finally, taking a deep breath. Anger welled up inside of her. She clinched her fist with a look that could pierce steel. She practiced using her new gifts. GES helped with her focus, and technique. She was strong, and worked hard to use her mind to summon, and control the world around her. She trained with warriors from the past learning as much as she could. Months had gone by, and she had forgotten the simple rule about time spent in the spirit world. GES had watched, and finally confronted her.

"It is time you return Spirit Walker!" GES tapped her staff upon the ground. A wave of energy trust outward hitting Nakoma.

"I'm coming for you chief!" Her body began to omit a great energy of blue flame. Her fists were clinched as she began to search for him with her new sight. Her body began to hover as the flames of blue shot from her eyes. Then she vanished, as GES picked up Bob and walked away.

CHAPTER 10

THE MEETING

Two days later at Lakota Hall-
The conference room was full of elders, from the three tribes of the reservation. Two of the chiefs from those tribes were there. There was Yampa Strong River of the Ute tribe, Chief Skybow of the Navajo tribe, and six other elders, two from each tribe. Samuel Red Cloud walked in, taking his position at the podium in the front of the room. There was a large video screen behind him.

"Welcome, my fellow chief's and elders, to Lakota Hall. If you would bring your attention to the big screen here behind me. You can witness what I have in my possession."

On the screen was an image of the Thunderbird in a cage, striking at every wall, trying to get out. It struck with so much force even the cameras that were several feet away shook.

"This is an outrage, Chief Red Cloud! You toy with the gods and kill anyone who gets in your way. You expect us to just sit by and let you control everything?" Chief Yampa said standing up from his chair. Accusing Samuel of his wrong doings.

"I'm trying to bring justice to our peoples, our culture, to everything the white man stole from us." Samuel said stepping from behind the podium and making his way to Yampa.

"What about Johnathan and Mary Standing Elk? They were good people, honest people. You had them killed!" Yampa pointed to Samuel in rage.

"Sacrifices are made to the betterment of our peoples." Samuel said as Yampa sat back down. Samuel pulled a Bowie knife and stuck it in the wood floor in front of Yampa.

"You're serious! To challenge me openly. You've gone mad with power." Yampa said, now standing back up.

"Yampa, we will not lose our heritage or our opportunity to stand tall. Now pick up the knife or I will." Samuel said ready for Yampa to make a move. The rest of the room fell silent as they sat in their chairs waiting for Yampa too make the first move.

Chief Skybow sat between the two. Rage was showing on his face. He was a close supporter of Red Cloud. Yampa showed fear as he faced Samuel. Sweat began to appear on his brow.

"You bring dishonor to your people. You're weak, and your tribe will be struck from the pages of history." Chief Skybow said, standing up to face Yampa.

"You cannot interfere with this challenge Chief Skybow." Elder Night Crow said as he to now stood up from his chair.

"Do you have a problem with my challenge, Yampa? Do you, Chief Red Cloud?" Skybow said turning to look at both men.

Samuel nodded in acceptance as Yampa lunged for the knife. Skybow shoved him to the floor. Yampa rolled to his left, scrambling to get to his feet. Skybow picked up the knife as Yampa charged. Skybow thrust the knife upward as Yampa came in. The knife pierced him just under the rib cage, through the liver and diaphragm. Yampa gasped for air as he grabbed Skybow by the shoulders. Yampa then fell to the floor dead. Skybow then scalped Yampa, wiping the blade off on Yampa's body. Holding up the scalp, Skybow than gave a war cry, that soon had the others joining in support. Samuel motioned to some security guards to remove the body. He made his way back to the podium. He raised his hand to quiet the group. "Thank you for your support. Who is the eldest of the Ute tribe?" Samuel said.

Benjamin Little Bear raised his hand, saying. "I am the eldest."

"Well, Chief Little Bear, do I have your support?" Samuel said, now looking at him.

"Yes, Chief Red Cloud." Little Bear said covering his heart with his right fist.

"If you look here at the harness, you will see that there is where the spirit of the Thunderbird is kept. It transforms it's host into the weapon that it is. My goal is to help the host gain control of the spirit and utilize it for our people." Samuel said, pointing to the screen.

"Is that your son?" Chief Skybow asked now sitting back down in his chair and placing the knife on the table.

"My son was chosen, yes. Whether it was by fate or by accident is of no consequence. What is important is getting him to control the spirit of the Thunderbird, helping him control his calling." Samuel said, looking at Skybow.

"Trying to control the spirit of a god is a slippery slope, Chief Red Cloud." Elder Night Crow said looking more concerned but still eagerly listening.

"Which is why my research team will be working around the clock to test and aid my son."

"How do you expect to control such power? That is the question because from the fables, the Thunderbird destroys everything in it's path." Elder Night Crow said, now leaning forward in his chair.

"Tesla created his coils and were brought here to this area in the 1900's. Tesla himself understood that by harnessing the power of the Thunderbird he could produce an endless supply of electricity to everyone for free."

"You're saying Tesla knew about the Thunderbird not being a myth?" Elder Night Crow said, now intrigued.

"Like anything we try to accomplish in life. You must have faith and believe. This is just the first of many my, brothers. The myths, the legends are real."

George, the bodyguard approached Samuel and whispered in his ear. Samuel nodded and George left the room.

"I'm sorry, gentlemen. I have another matter that requires my immediate attention. If anyone would like a tour later on, please don't hesitate to call my secretary."

Samuel left the room with George close behind. They headed to the house he was staying in. The home was a huge cabin. It was more like a picturesque scene from a magazine to say the least. Six bedrooms, four bath, cabin and an attached four car garage. There was a circular drive, in front around a fountain. In the center of the fountain was a metal ram standing on a rock. As they arrived police detective Lane was waiting in the drive with several local tribal police and Lou.

"I have to say, Detective Lane, you are persistent." Samuel said, getting out of the black van.

"I have video proof that your son arrived at the hotel and never left. I also have video footage of a black panel van registered to you leaving the area of a fire." Detective Lane said, knowing he had Samuel dead to rights.

"Detective, before the wheels in your head go too much faster, know this. That you are standing on tribal lands. You came alone, which is the biggest mistake anyone can make in your line of work. So, I'm going to say this. You work for me now. I'll pay you generously, of course. You just have to creatively write your way out of my dealings." Samuel said.

"Did you just threaten me, Mr. Red Cloud?" Detective Lane said, as too now he realized his mistake.

"Yes, I did, and if you wish to leave here alive, then I suggest you accept my offer."

Detective Lane started to reach for his gun, but all the tribal police, George and Lou drew their guns first. Detective Lane paused and raised his hands in surrender.

"Last chance, Detective Lane." Samuel said with a stern look. Samuel reached out his hand. Detective Lane brought his hand up to shake hands with him.

'Relax Detective, Oh yeah one more thing."

Just then, Lou hit the detective with an epee pen type syringe in the back of the neck.

"Ouch!" Detective Lane said as he reached for the back of his neck.

"Got to make sure you stay loyal. Can't have you trying anything stupid."

"What was that?" Detective Lane said.

"An explosive tracker. Some call it a slave tracker. Consider it my insurance policy that you do what I ask. George, pay him double the normal fee. We are going to stage an accident. I need your report writing skills to cover it all up." Samuel said, turning away from the group and proceeding to the house.

Detective Lane rubbed his neck again, looking at the men before him. He slowly turned to his car moving to leave.

"I suggest you don't come back to the res." George said as he walked slowly behind the detective.

Detective Lane got into his car and nodded in compliance to George. The other men holstered their weapons as he drove off. As he moved further away, he kept checking his rearview mirror to see if they followed. No one was following. He rubbed his neck again knowing that he was compromised.

CHAPTER 11

PICKING UP THE PIECES

— **wo** months later.
Nakoma stood at the spot where her father had
died, looking at the blood stain still on the ground. Then
she looked up to see the remains of what had once been
her home. Bob the cat rubbed up against her leg and,
trotted off toward the house. She began to cry again as
the two beads became lights again, and then turned into
the shapes of her parents.

"Don't cry, dear. We are with you." Her mother said.

"No, you're not, physically, He took you from me."
Nakoma said as the anger welled up inside.

"Anger is not the answer. Look what happened to me."
Her father said, pointing to the ground where his body
had been.

"I just want my life back. I want you here. I want it the
way it was." Nakoma said, punching the ground as she fell
to her knees. She took the head dress off. Her parents
vanished. She looked at the headdress in anger, and hate
filled her heart. She threw the headdress toward the
destroyed house. Within a few minutes, a truck came
down the drive. Nakoma came to her feet, wiping away the

tears. It was Tim Dobbson, her godparent, coming in his fire station truck. When she saw him get out, she began to cry more. Tim rushed over to her, giving her a hug.

"I'm sorry, kid!" Tim said as he just continued to hold her. Minutes went by, and then Bob the cat came back to Nakoma. The headdress had taken form into a collar around his neck. He brushed up against her and then Tim's, causing them to separate long enough to recognize him.

"Hey, Bob, that's a cool collar you got on." Tim said as he reached down to pick him up.

"Yeah, he's all that's left of my life." Nakoma said, still angry and crying. Hoping Tim didn't pay too much attention to the collar.

"Wow, that hurts, you know. Your father and mother were my friends. Your father was a brother to me. He's helped me more than I can count. I'm going to honor him by being here for you." Tim said, grabbing Nakoma for another hug, squishing Bob between them.

"I'm sorry, Tim. It's just that they're gone." Nakoma began to cry again, taking Bob from his arms.

"I know, kid! I miss them too." Tim just stood there looking at Nakoma in her brokenness, remembering when his wife and son had been taken by a drunk driver just eight years ago. The feelings came back to him, and he grabbed Nakoma for another hug.

"Where have you been? We searched everywhere for you. Yesterday the tribe came and moved the livestock. They took the equipment for auction, last month." Tim said now wondering where she truly was.

"I don't know. What day is it?" Nakoma asked trying to get her bearings of how long she had been in the spirit world.

'It's Monday, August 3rd. You've been gone for two months. You know what? Let's not worry about that right now. Let's get you in the truck. You can stay with me for a while." Tim said as he side stepped to let Nakoma walk by to the truck.

The two of them, along with Bob got into the truck and drove away. The drive to his home was about fifteen minutes away. It was the longest time either of them had spent together, without a word being spoken. As Tim pulled into the parking spot, Bob the cat meowed at Nakoma.

"Yes, Bob, this is our new home for now." Nakoma said, petting his fur.

Bob slipped off the collar and patted it with his paw. Nakoma just smiled. "No, you wear it for right now." Nakoma said, petting his fur some more.

"Come on, kid, let me show you your room." Tim got out and walked to the front door, searching for the right key.

Nakoma got out of the truck and made her way up the steps of his single wide trailer. It was a god-awful lime green color with two pink flamingos on either side of the steps. All in all, it was in good shape for an eighties-style trailer, but it was an eyesore for the whole trailer park. Once inside, Nakoma was surprised to see that Tim maintained his home very well. Tim looked back at Nakoma as she checked out the layout.

"Come on now, kid. Your room is over here. I've been going through the debris of your place the last couple of months. I was able to find some suitable belongings."

Tim pointed to the room, and Nakoma made her way inside. She looked upon some clothes and items that he had been able to gather. A photo album, her father's shotgun, and some smaller Knick knacks that her mother had.

'Thanks, Tim!" Nakoma said as she looked at all that remained of her home.

"Well, when you're ready, we can go to town and get you some things."

"I want my dad's horse, Tim!" Nakoma said as she turned and looked at him.

"Nakoma, I can't keep a horse here." Tim said, looking at her with sadness.

"I'll keep him at the stables on the res." Nakoma said, looking at Tim to acknowledge the fact or idea.

"Okay, okay! Calm down. I'll make some calls." Tim said, knowing she needed the hope.

"Thank you, and sorry. It's important." Nakoma said cracking a half hearten smile.

"I get it. No apologies needed." Tim said as he left the doorway, giving Nakoma her space. Bob hopped up on to the bed, and Nakoma took the collar off of him. She turned it back into the bracelet and placed it on her left wrist. Hours passed as Nakoma sat going through the photo album. Tim knocked on the door of her room.

"You hungry? I got pizza coming. Pineapple and ham." Tim said with a straight face.

"Ewww. Seriously? Tim that's not pizza. How could you?" Nakoma said with disgust.

"Gotcha!" Tim said with a laugh, pointing at her. Nakoma threw a pillow at him, losing her balance and falling off the bed. Tim just laughed as she scrambled to her feet. Tim ran to the living room. Nakoma gave chase. The doorbell rang. Tim trotted over to the door, grabbing his wallet from his back pocket.

"Damn! Nakoma, can you get that? I'll be right back." Tim ran to the back bedroom to grab money. Nakoma went to the front door and answered it.

"Nakoma! You're alive!" The young man said, holding a pizza and smiling from ear to ear.

"Hey, Pete, Yeah, I'm fine." Nakoma said with a half-hearted smile, but it quickly faded.

Pete Stanton was a year behind Nakoma in school. He was tall at about six two and skinny as a rail. A face full of acne and braces. A real big dork to most. He would always stop and stare at her. She knew he did, but it never bothered her. Boys always stared at her. Pete just seemed harmless and backwards.

"Sorry about your folks." Pete said, handing her the pizza.

"Thanks, Pete. Hey, could you not tell anyone you saw me? I need time, you know."

"Yeah, sure, anything for you.' Pete said with a smile.

"Thanks, Pete." Nakoma said, as she grabbed the pizza.

Tim came up with the money. "Well, her you go son and an extra ten for your tip."

"Thank you, sir. And don't worry, Nakoma. I won't say nothing." Pete said as he took the money from Tim, smiling at her.

Pete left, and Nakoma closed the door. She gave a small smile as she went and sat on the edge of the couch smelling the pizza. Tim took the pizza and held it up to his nose.

"Ah, pineapple and ham. Let's eat." Tim said with a smile.

"You're kidding, right? You better be kidding, Tim." Nakoma said, springing up from the couch. Tim ran to the kitchen with the pizza, and Nakoma chased him. Tim got to the counter, trying to cover the pizza by blocking her. She reached with her left hand and Tim noticed the bracelet.

"Hey where did you get that?" Tim said, backing away from the pizza and looking at her wrist.

"I got it at the exhibit when I went to the university, It's nothing really." Nakoma said trying to hide it behind her.

"Well, I think it's cool!" Tim said as he opened the pizza box, smiling at Nakoma.

"Supreme!" Nakoma smiled back, punching Tim in the arm.

Tim grabbed some paper plates as Nakoma took the pizza over to the dining table. They sat and ate with very little to say. Tim knew that there was foul play in Johnathon and Mary's deaths. But what caused him more wonder is where Nakoma had been. Had she been hiding or was she a part of it? In his heart and soul, he knew she was innocent. He didn't have the guts to ask. All he knows right now is that she is alive and safe.

CHAPTER 12

TEST 135

"Chief Red Cloud, we are ready to conduct test 135. Everything so far has been unsuccessful." Dr. Baysinger said, awaiting a response from Samuel.

"Do it!" Samuel said, looking out the window of the observation booth they were in.

"Trying to reach your son through visual stimulus may work." Dr. Kim Baysinger said, glancing over at Samuel before she activated the test. Video screens came on all around the box that the Thunderbird was caged in. The screens began to show slides of photos and home videos of Jeromia's childhood. Photos of his mom and friends seem to draw his attention. The Thunderbird would turn his head and body, looking at the screens.

"Put it in the box now!" Samuel said as he motioned through the window.

A scientist down on the ground floor nodded and grabbed the football. He walked on over to the cage and opened a small door putting the football into the cage with the Thunderbird. The Thunderbird screamed at the scientist and came toward the football. He picked up the football. Then a segment of video played with his mother telling him to come inside. The Thunderbird stopped and looked at the screens, turning it's head in curiosity.

"Jeromia, sweety, it's time to come in."

"Loop that part!" Samuel said, motioning to Dr. Baysinger.

The Thunderbird screamed and then dropped to one knee still clutching the football. The wings and tail feathers started to recede. His legs began to change back into regular form. Lightning surrounded him like a dome. The Thunderbird then placed his right hand on the ground. Within a minute, Jeromia was back to himself, lying on the floor still holding the football. He was exhausted. It appeared to take a toll on his body.

"I want that audio looped and create some digitally. We found a chink in the armor." Samuel said, grinning in knowing he found something.

"Mom, I'm coming!" Jeromia said, tired and delirious as he tried to rise but fell back down never letting go of the football.

"Get the team in there with a chip. I will control him." Samuel told Dr. Baysinger. She looked at him with concern.

"I don't think it's ready for human trials, sir!" Dr. Baysinger said looking uneasy with his decision.

"It is now, and don't ever question me again, Dr. Baysinger." Samuel said in anger.

"Yes, sir!" Dr. Baysinger grabbed the back of her neck. Just then Lou came into the room.

"Chief, Dr. Fleming is leaving in a hurry and just got to her car. Also, Detective Lane is here as you requested."

"Track her for now. See who she calls and where she goes. Send up the detective." Samuel said, now looking out the windows of the observation tower.

Lou went back down and escorted Detective Lane up to the top of the observation tower in the warehouse where Samuel was waiting.

"What are you doing, Red Cloud? Is that your son?" Detective Lane said, horrified of what he was witnessing.

"Come, Detective Lane. The explosion at the warehouse was no minor accident. My son placed the ancient harness of the Thunderbird on himself in a drunken stupor that night at the hotel." Samuel said as he played back the footage of the last test performed.

"What in god's name is going on here?" Detective Lane backed up a few feet, bumping into Lou.

"Like I said, Detective Lane, I need your help. I will pay you well, but my matters cannot be public. My son and his friend were driving drunk when his car lost control and veered off a cliff. My son is in critical condition and in a coma. His friend, on the other hand did not make it." Samuel said, instructing the detective in his role.

"This is insane! How is this even possible?" Detective Lane said, stepping away from Lou.

"Look, write it down and focus." Samuel said, now facing the detective.

"Yes, sir!" Detective Lane said, fumbling for his notebook. Detective Lane grabbed his notebook and began to write what he was told, looking periodically at the screen of the test run on Red Cloud's son.

"My son was moved here on the reservation for closer observation after his accident. His friend was pronounced dead at the scene."

"You killed a student?" Detective Lane said, looking up at Samuel in shock.

"Detective Lane, focus or I will find someone who will." Samuel said, now getting irritated.

"Yes, sir!" Detective Lane said, looking back at his notebook.

"I want your creative writing skills in the paper tonight. Understood?" Samuel said, taking a step forward.

"Sir, Dr. Fleming has stopped and made a phone call to this number. It belongs to a Kimberly Fisher. She's a reporter for the..." Dr. Baysinger said, looking at a monitor.

"Are you tracking her?" Samuel said, turning to the monitor.

"Yes, sir, she is en route to her now." Dr. Baysinger said, pointing to the screen.

"What is this? You're tracking phones for GPS. That's government-type stuff. Am I right? How did you get this?" Detective Lane said, moving closer to the monitor.

"Watch and learn detective. The tracker I put on you is a slave chip like the one in Dr. Fleming. When you don't do as I ask, this will be the result." Samuel said as he stepped back to let Detective Lane have a better look.

"She has arrived at her location, sir." Lou said holding a tablet. He then handed it to Samuel.

"Bring it up on the screen here. In the middle. Full satellite image." Samuel said. Dr. Baysinger brought it up on the screen.

"Call her here on the HUD." Samuel said, trying to give her one last chance.

"The phone rang but went to voicemail." Dr. Baysinger said, looking to Samuel.

"I tried to give you a chance, doctor." Samuel said with disappointment.

"Sir, the area is clear, no other heat signatures on the satellite scan. We are clear for the execution." Lou said, as Samuel pushed the button on the tablet in his hands. The signal died, and the heat signatures faded from the screen. Detective Lane grabbed the back of his neck. Fear came across his face.

"Well, detective now there is another scene for you to clean up." Samuel said, handing the tablet to Lou.

"Yes, sir! I'm on my way." Detective Lane said, making his way out of the warehouse quickly.

"Sir, the sweep teams are en route for clean up." Dr. Baysinger said, glancing at Samuel.

"Very good. When he wakes call me." Samuel said as he left the room.

Samuel left after the detective, leaving the warehouse. He made his way to Lakota Hall. Once he arrived, he made his way to the conference room. Inside, Chief Skybow, and Chief Little Bear awaited. They stood as he entered.

"Please have a seat, gentlemen. My time has been averted, and I need you two to step up. Chief Little Bear, you are going to take over casino operations along with the reservation needs. You will only take fifteen percent of profit. Chief Skybow, you will handle security of the reservation and any strike teams needed. You will also handle cleanup when directed. Do I make myself clear gentlemen?" Samuel said, looking at them.

Both the men nodded in acknowledgement. Samuel stood up, and the two men followed suit. He left the room as the two men stood looking at each other smiling. It was the first time that Chief Red Cloud had trusted anyone with such responsibilities. They were happy to have the trust. Samuel left Lakota Hall and went to his home there on the reservation.

CHAPTER 13
VISIONS

Tim stood at Nakoma's door and cracked it open with a low knock.

"Hey, I've got to go to work, kid! So just hang out, and I will call the res. for your horse." Tim said, knowing she wasn't ready to go back to school. Moreover, he wasn't ready to try to explain things either. Let alone he hasn't asked where she's been the last couple of months.

"Thanks Tim!" Nakoma said as she rolled over in her bed. Bob the cat darted out the room towards the living room.

"Okay then. We'll talk later, okay?" Tim said, stepping away from the door.

Nakoma just gave a thumbs up in compliance, and Tim left the doorway. He was worried but knew she needed time. Tim left for work, making plans to get back to Nakoma's home to find out what happened. He knew there was foul play involved. He also knew the res. wouldn't take kindly to an outsider sticking their nose into their business. The big concern for Tim was that if it was foul play, then they would be coming for Nakoma next.

Later that morning, Tim called the reservation stables, giving inquiry to the status of the livestock of the Standing Elk family. He was not well received as the man on the other end hung up on him. Nakoma finally dragged her butt out of bed at around ten in the morning because Bob would not leave her alone.

"Okay, Bob, I'll let you out, but don't go far. What do you mean you took a shit in Tim's fern? Bob! Come, on let's go." Nakoma said, getting out of bed in a hurry.

It was the first time that she had communicated telepathically without even realizing it. Nakoma made her way to the kitchen, crinkling her nose to the smell of fresh cat shit. She opened the back sliding door of the trailer, and Bob ran out. Nakoma grabbed the fern and set it out on the back patio table. The patio was fenced in with wood about six foot high and a small gate at the east end of it. There was no grass, as the landscaping was filled with rock around the patio. Small steps led to the gate. Nakoma made her way back into the kitchen. She heated up some of the leftover pizza. Once she was done eating, she noticed an old newspaper on a little table next to the front door. She went and grabbed it, making her way back to the kitchen table. *Twelve Dead in Meth Lab Fire* was the headline of the front page. Just then, an old Ford pickup truck came driving by. It was a red and white two-tone, two Native men driving really slow by the trailer. The engine had a real bad miss, making a ticking sound as it idled by. The exhaust had been cut out, making it sound more like the truck was chocking than aggressive. Nakoma paid it no real mind as she continued to read about the fire. Once she was done, she placed the paper back on to the small table where she found it. She went back out to the patio to get Bob. As she exited the back door, she heard the truck again. Bob began to hiss and raise the hair on his back. Nakoma got scared. She removed the bracelet and thought of the headdress. It became the headdress. She put it on, grabbing Bob and thinking of the spirit world. Instantly, she was there.

"Illuminate!"

"Welcome back, Spirit Walker!" GES said as she stood in front of Nakoma with a blank expression on her face.

"What now, GES? I'm really not in the mood." Nakoma said letting Bob onto the ground, and he ran off to go play.

"I know you are hurting, Spirit Walker. I want you to come with me to the Elder Tree." GES said, reaching down and picking up Bob as he came by.

"He's my cat, GES. Don't even think about keeping him." Nakoma said, stomping her foot in frustration and then following behind GES as she walked off with Bob.

"Come along, Spirit Walker. It is time for you to meet her." GES said, still holding Bob and walking down a trail by the stream.

Nakoma could tell it would be several miles to the tree. For she could see for miles just in the area they were in. The stream ran past them on their left. There were already many trees and plants. All had the beautiful hue of blue. Little spirit orbs danced all around. Some would come in close to her face and then dart off. They were approaching a hill, and Nakoma thought about it. She tele- ported to the top of the hill. She laughed a little, knowing she could do it with ease. Nakoma looked back at GES holding Bob, and then she turned around to see the area.

Nakoma's eyes widened, and jaw dropped with amazement at the valley. It was like there was a hidden world before her. She could see the tree. It was huge and covered in blue leaves. It looked twenty stories high and a mile wide. It's trunk was white, and the stream ran through the center. The whole area was lit up like a beautiful sunny day. GES walked by Nakoma, giggling at her now realizing her new world. Nakoma could also tell it was about four miles to the tree. She picked a spot in front of the tree, and instantly she was there. She stood in astonishment at it's beauty. GES walked by her and went into the tree.

"How?" Nakoma said in amazement.

"Much to learn, you have., Now come along." GES said as she went into what appeared to be an entrance of a carved-out section. Nakoma could now hear voices, and then a voice she has never heard before spoke to her.

"Come, child, let us see what awaits you."

It was peaceful in it's tone. Nakoma proceeded to enter the tree. Once inside, she could see it was even more beautiful. There was a pool in the center of the area. The stream moved away from the pool. The stream itself was about eight feet wide, and the pool was approximately forty feet in diameter. Vines hung from the top of the area looking like Christmas lights on a house. Nakoma was still several thousands of yards away from the pool. Above the pool, there were vines wrapped around one big orb of light. It seemed to be the one calling her. Nakoma thought of the edge of the pool, and she was there. Stones began to rise up out of the water, creating a path to the center. In the center rose a stone about eight feet in diameter. Nakoma stepped up on to the rocks, making her way to the center. When she was there, she looked up and saw the stone. It wasn't a light at all. It was like the stone she wore on her headdress, but it was as big as she was, wrapped in vines above the pool and looking more like a grand chandelier in a mansion.

"There you are. My, how you have grown. Strong, driven, and passionate. These are good qualities of a Spirit Walker." The stone said as Nakoma approached.

"Who are you?" Nakoma asked, looking at it's beauty.

"Who do you say I am?" The stone said.

"GES said the Elder Tree, but you have a stone like mine. The aura you omit is good, loving, and nurturing, but also harsh at times. I feel you are... Gaia!" Nakoma said with a smile

"Correct! I was created to sustain the earth's life so that it's inhabitants can live." Gaia said

"But your stone is like mine! Where do they come from?" Nakoma asked, looking more intently at the stone.

"The heavens cast down the stones in it's creation. Man found them and learned they had great power. Most of the ones used in the early days were used to gain power and influence. Your culture used them to rule or protect the lands. Yours was created to guard the world against evil, same as such the Thunderbird. But I feel one of your kind is going to twist him to do great evil." Gaia said, and the colors of the stone changed for a moment.

"Chief Red Cloud!" Nakoma said as anger started to build.

"Yes, but enough of that for now. Hold still and let's see your future." Gaia said.

Nakoma stood still as vines came down and encased her like a cocoon, raising her above the pool. Then the pool of water turned to flame all around her. She was unaware of what was happening as she fell into a sleep. All her memories came crashing in from her past. Then it changed again. Images of her fighting the Thunderbird and then many other creatures. A minator, demons, werewolves and the windigo. Then she saw herself and a man of gold hovering over her in the sky. He was bright as the sun. Then she felt the heat from his power and began to burn. Pain ran through her body. Light began to pierce the cocoon that held her. Nakoma screamed as the light shot out from her like an energy of great force. The cocoon exploded, and Nakoma hovered in the air. Energy surrounded her, then she spoke.

"I am the Spirit Walker!" Nakoma's voice rang out with authority and power. Nakoma then looked down at GES holding Bob. She smiled at them than vanished.

"Go, little Spirit Walker. Fulfill your destiny." GES said, putting Bob onto the ground. Nakoma appeared at the stables on the reservation. She walked up to her father's horse in a nearby corral. A young man turned around and saw her. He approached, wondering why she was wearing traditional attire.

"Hey there, Can I help you?" The young man said, seeing her standing by the horse.

Nakoma turned around. Her eyes were glowing blue like flames. And then she spoke with a haunting voice.

"This horse is mine now and tell Chief Red Cloud I'm coming for him!" Nakoma said.

The young man fell backward in fear trying to get away. She touched the horse, and they vanished before his eyes. Nakoma and her father's horse teleported back to the spirit world. She patted him on the shoulder and scratched him behind the left ear.

"Go. Be ready when I call." Nakoma said as the horse took off into the field by the tree.

"It's good that you have him, but he along with Bob cannot stay here. They need the real world to sustain them." GES said to her as a warning.

"I know, GES! I must find Red Cloud. He will pay for what he has done. Just watch them for a while."

Nakoma vanished again.

CHAPTER 14
SIGNING DAY!

The following Monday-

Other than being the Spirit Walker, Nakoma was a well-established female athlete within the state. She was also a straight A student. Today, she would be accepting the college of her choosing at the high school gym. She appeared back in her room at Tim's. A few moments later, she heard Tim's truck pulling up. She removed the head-dress and turned it back into the bracelet. She put it on her left wrist and walked to the living room.

"Nakoma! Sorry I'm late. Shift change took longer than expected this morning. Grab your stuff. Let's get you to school." Tim said as he walked to the kitchen to grab a bagel.

"Hey, where's my fern?" Tim said, searching the room for it.

"Oh, sorry Tim, Bob kind of used it as a litter box. So, I put it outside on the patio so it wouldn't stink up the trailer." Nakoma said with a shoulder shrug and smile.

"Thanks, I guess. I'll get a litter box for him after I drop you off at school." Tim said as he crinkled his face a little.

"I don't feel like going." Nakoma said, worried about all that people might say.

"You have to, Nakoma! Today, you sign with Colorado University! You are going to CU, right? I mean your father was a huge CU fan and I'm a CU fan. Please let it be CU!" Tim said, closing his eyes and crossing his fingers. Then he opened one eye at Nakoma. She looked at him with a scowl on her face.

"What, I'm just saying..." Tim said, anticipating her answer. Nakoma still stood looking at him, then she smiled.

"Yes, I'm signing with CU!" Nakoma said, spinning around in her mother's favorite sun dress.

"Yes!" Tim said as he jumped into the air.

"It would honor him and my family." Nakoma said, smiling.

Tim just smiled and realized suddenly that she had the entire world on her shoulders. He kept his smile, but the worry in his eyes showed he understood.

"Come on, then. Let's go get you to school. I like the dress!" Tim said, heading to the door.

The two left the trailer, getting into his truck. They drove off toward the high school. A mile down the road, they came to a stop sign. Nakoma could hear the truck from yesterday coming from behind. Her eyes widened as she looked back. It was the same two men.

"That truck sounds like shit!" Tim said as he, too looked in the rear-view mirror. Nakoma closed her eyes as she focused on the driver.

"Let me see!" Nakoma said as she rubbed the stone on her wrist with the palm of her right hand. Instantly, she was seeing through the driver's eyes, and she could hear their conversation.

"I say we kill her now. Chief will cover it up for us. Maybe promote us." The passenger said, looking at the driver.

"We are to follow and report. The chief was clear in his instructions. Crossing him will be certain death." The driver said.

Nakoma could now see they were passing a farm with cattle on the left. She tried to give a thought to the driver to slow down as they were too close. The same as she had done with David and Debbie that night in the motel. The driver did slow down giving her a chance. She began to summon the herd into the roadway. The herd moved fast, rushing through the fence and into the middle of the road between the two trucks.

"Wow. Did you see that? Maybe we should stop and help." Tim said as he hit the brakes for a moment.

"No! We are already running late. I have to prepare for my signing." Nakoma said, trying to convince him to go.

"Yes, you're right and don't get upset if people look at you differently." Tim said showing concern.

"Why? Cause my family and best friend are dead?" Nakoma said staring to get angry.

"Hmm... Yes! I'm sorry Nakoma, I just..." Tim said with a loss of words.

"I know Tim, I'll be okay, It's just hard." Nakoma said, now looking out the passenger window.

"Hey, hey you'll do fine. You're the bravest most courageous girl uhm..., young woman I know. If anyone can stand up to this world after getting knocked down, is you." Tim said, trying to inspire her.

'Thanks, Tim!" Nakoma smiled and then turned her gaze out the passenger window in thought. They arrived to the school twenty minutes later. Nakoma got out of the truck. Her fellow students all stopped to stare.

"I'll pick you up after school." Tim said, leaning to the passenger side to look at Nakoma.

"No, I'll catch a ride later with a friend." Nakoma said back with a smirk.

"As you wish!" Tim sat back up in his seat, tapping his right hand on the steering wheel.

Tim drove away as Nakoma stood on the side walk looking at the school. Her classmates stared and whispered, as Principal Lin came out front and Nakoma began to walk inside. It was like a walk of shame to her, as everyone whispered.

"Excuse me, ladies and gentlemen, get to your classes. Come on now." Principal Lin said, rushing them and seeing that Nakoma was walking with her head held high.

"Nakoma it's good to see you this morning. Are you sure..." Principal Lin said as Nakoma cut her short.

"I'm fine ma'am." She walked by continuing to hold her head high.

"Good. After lunch we will be set up in the gymnasium for your signing. I am sorry for your loss." I've made accommodations to your teachers for your makeup work." Principal Lin said with sympathy as Nakoma walked by. Nakoma nodded and proceeded into the school.

Tony Arjun, the driver and, the passenger, Frank Dunken, were in the red and white two-tone truck near the school. Tony made a call to Chief Red Cloud.

"Sir, the girl is in the school, and the firefighter is gone."

"Don't stay there. You'll only draw attention to yourselves. Follow him see where he goes." Samuel said. Then he hung up the phone.

"Yes Sir!" Tony said. Then he looked at the phone, realizing he had been hung up on.

"What did he say, Tony?" Frank said, looking at the kids going into the school.

"We are to follow the firefighter." Tony said, putting the truck into drive and leaving the area.

The two men caught back up with Tim. They kept their distance as they noticed he was pulling into the Standing Elk ranch. They drove to the top of a hill nearby to get a better look of the area and watch.

"Dammit, Johnathon! What a mess you left me." Tim said as he slammed his fist into the steering wheel. He sat there for several hours until he fell asleep in the truck.

"How long is he going to sit there, Tony?"

"I don't know, Frank. We are to just follow and report. Standing Elk was his best friend. He's probably in mourning." Tony said, gripping the steering wheel with his hands.

"We could send him to meet him instead of hanging out here all day." Frank shifted in his seat, agitated with just watching.

"No, Frank!" Tony smacked the steering wheel with his hands.

"He's on the res. And he's a waseju. No one would judge us. People get missing all the time on the res." Frank said, looking out the door's window.

"No, Frank, That's enough!" Tony looked at him, ready to punch him in the mouth.

"Ah...I'm going to sleep. Wake me if we get to actually do something." Frank slouched in the seat, crossing his arms and closing his eyes.

"Fine. At least you'll be quiet." Frank shifted his weight to the left, leaning out the window of the driver door. Within a couple of hours, both men were asleep.

Throughout the morning, Nakoma could hear the whispers from everyone. She knew she had to keep it together even though every ounce of her being wanted to scream *enough*. Lunch came, and she sat alone at first. Then Pete Stanton came and sat at her table.

"Hey, Nakoma. Mind if I sit with you?" Pete said with sadness in his eyes.

"Thanks, Pete. No, I don't mind." Nakoma said, looking at her food and twirling her fork in some Jell-o.

"Sorry about your folks. My mom died when I was eight from cancer. It was hard at first, and I still miss her." Pete rambled on the whole lunch hour, trying to make Nakoma feel more at ease. He was a kind soul even though most of the kids here at school bullied him for being a half-blood. Nakoma tuned him out, focusing on the stares and whispers thrown her way. No one would question her for spending time with someone like Pete. Most of all now thinking she was still in mourning.

"So, when I saw you at the trailer... Who are you staying with?" Pete asked, and then took a drink of his milk.

"A family friend, and that stays between us, Pete, okay?" Nakoma said, now looking at Pete with seriousness in her face.

"Okay, but..."

"I need you to promise me, Pete. I also need you to find out places that Red Cloud has with lots of security. White coats coming in and out, possibly. Don't be too nosy, though, and get caught. Let me see your phone." Pete handed her his phone. Nakoma put her phone number into Pete's phone under "Lacrosse Girl." Pete just smiled as no girl had ever given him her number.

"But why?" Pete asked, now wondering what could be so bad.

"There are bad things happening, Pete, and Red Cloud is behind it." Nakoma said, looking him the eyes.

"Why not tell the police?" Pete asked, trying to understand the mystery she was in.

"He's paid them off and don't believe the news. My parents were killed by him. I am going to find out what he's up to." Nakoma said, looking throughout the lunchroom.

"Oh...okay, Nakoma. Spy games, mission impossible." Pete was staring off towards the ceiling, smiling.

"Pete, I'm serious. This is serious." Nakoma stared into his face as Pete's smile faded to fear.

"Okay, Nakoma!" Pete answered, now looking at his lunch like a whipped dog.

'Thanks, Pete!" Nakoma got up, giving a kiss on the cheek. Then she made her way to the gymnasium. Principal Lin waved to her as she came in. Nakoma made her way up to her where there was a table set up with microphones and a couple of chairs. Mrs. Harris, her coach was there as well. Reporters from across the state and some from the across the country stood taking photos and raising their hands. Nakoma centered herself behind the table. Sports analyst Brian Scott spoke out first.

"With the recent passing of your parents, do you feel this is the right time to make such a decision?"

"Who are you?" Nakoma said, getting angry at the heartless question, but she had expected it.

"Sorry, Brian Scott with ESPN. I write for the national lacrosse teams. So, your thoughts, Ms. Standing Elk?"

"My father was a rancher on the reservation. Third generation of my family, and he was revered with honor and respect among our people. Though it is hard, and, yes quite untimely for most, but life can always change in an instant, whether you're ready for it or not. As I make my decision today, it is with that honor and respect that my father and mother gave me. It is with this honor of my family I choose to go to Colorado University, where I will major in history and minor in science. Thank you all for coming."

Nakoma left the gymnasium as Principal Lin tried to stop her with tears running down her face. Cameras flashed and video cameras continued to roll watching her leave. Principal Lin quickly followed behind her.

"Nakoma, Nakoma...Nakoma Standing Elk!" Principal Lin yelled to her, stopping just outside the gym doors. Nakoma stopped, turning to face Ms. Lin. Tears were flowing down her face. Principal Lin was crying too has she walked up and hugged her.

"I'm so sorry, Nakoma!" Principal said, crying even more as she pulled back to look at Nakoma.

"I'll be fine, Ms. Lin, really!" Nakoma said as tears ran down her face. She wiped them with her forearm.

"No, sweetheart, you're not fine, and it shows. Please take the rest of the day off. I'll tell your teachers to assign you to e-learning. I'll also make sure they give you extra time." Principal Lin said, trying to give Nakoma some peace about coming to school.

"Yes, Ms. Lin, and thank you. I have to go to the restroom to freshen up." Nakoma said as she turned and walked away.

"Please, dear, come back when you're ready. We will be waiting with open arms." Principal Lin said trying to wipe away her tears.

Nakoma proceeded to the restroom. When she entered, she checked the area to make sure it was clear. She was alone, and she went and stood in front of the mirror by the sinks. She removed the bracelet and turned it into the headdress in a thought. She placed the headdress on her head and vanished. The janitor, James Longbow, came in, knocking, and saw Nakoma vanish. He rubbed his eyes and shook his head in disbelief. He pulled a small whiskey bottle from his jacket, taking a drink and rubbing his eyes again.

"I should have stayed home!" He wiped his mouth with his sleeve, wondering if his mind was playing tricks on him or if he had too much to drink.

CHAPTER 15

LOCKS OF LOVE

Nakoma appeared in the spirit world. She sat on a rock and began crying some more by the stream. A blue orb of light flew up to her, dancing in front of her eyes. Suddenly, it started to take shape. Nakoma looked up as she appeared. She was beautiful with long dark hair like hers. Her dress was long and ceremonial of her Native culture. Beads adorned the hide dress around the shoulders and down the sides. She had two turkey feathers on the left tied into her hair.

"Who are you?" Nakoma said, wiping away her tears.

"I am Pocahontas, Spirit Walker. You have a long journey ahead of you. Your focus is needed now more than ever."

"Focus, really! Everything I cared for is gone. I can't do this alone." Nakoma said, now getting mad.

"You're not alone, Spirit Walker." Pocahontas said, smiling.

Just then her father, mother, grandfather, grandmother, Debbie, and GES with Bob appeared. Bob ran over to her lap. She stroked his fur as she looked up at them.

"What you ask is too much. I didn't want this. Not for what it has cost me." Nakoma stood up in anger. Pocahontas just smiled.

"I loved once, too; you know. I gave up everything for that love. I had a chance to see great things in my time. I left my people for the adventure of love. Even though I followed my heart, I never forgot who I was. Memories are yours to keep, share, and grow upon. The price that you have paid now will be yours tenfold in return. What I'm saying is don't stop your love. Let it grow to something bigger. So big that the earth shakes in it's presence. Your strength is your courage. You will stand when the fear is great. Your love for this world will shine brighter than the sun."

"I have to find him! But I can't see him." Nakoma said trying to focus on Jeromia.

"Wards have been placed to keep you out. Red Cloud is smart, but you are smarter Spirit Walker." GES said, placing a hand on Nakoma's left arm.

"You love him! I see it now. I've felt that love before and it is like no other. Do not mis lead Pete in your journey. He is young and to naive to understand. He will be useful to you." Pocahontas said, then she turned back into a spirit orb.

"You are my granddaughter, and you are stronger than the world. More beautiful than anyone deserves. You bring honor to us all. You are now the Spirit Walker, and you must find the fortitude and strength to overcome." Her grandfather said, puffing out his chest in pride. Then he too turned back into a spirit orb.

"We will always be with you and here when you need us." Her mother said as she turned into a spirit orb along with her father. Debbie just smiled and turned into an orb as well.

Nakoma felt a new confidence within herself. She smiled as the orbs of light danced in front of her. GES picked Bob back up and stood watching Nakoma.

"Thank you all, it was nice to meet you, Pocahontas. I must go now and stop Red Cloud." Nakoma teleported back to the restroom right before the janitor, James Longbow, came in. She removed the headdress and turned it back into the bracelet.

"My apologies, Nakoma. I thought everyone was in class. So sorry!"

"It's okay, Mr. Longbow I was just leaving." Nakoma left the restroom. James pulled the whiskey bottle from his jacket and took a drink.

"I'm getting too old for this shit!" He wondered if he could do the job as janitor.

Nakoma made her way to the office. She came to the receptionist, Darlene, who was playing on the computer at her desk.

"Where kind I find Pete Stanton?" Nakoma said leaning on the counter. One of the teacher assistants, Julie Daksha, chimed in.

"Pete the Stick is in study hall this period. He's a total loser, if you ask me." She said, acting like a portentous snob.

"I wasn't asking, you snob. Pete is a good person!" Nakoma turned toward her, ready to punch her in the face.

"Girls! That's enough!" Principal Lin said as she walked back into the office. Darlene sat in shock as Julie stormed off.

"Detention Saturday, Ms. Daksha! 9:00 a.m.! Now what do you want with Pete?" Principle Lin pointed at Julie, then turned back toward Nakoma.

"I need him to give me a ride home. Or Tim's house!" Nakoma relaxed her hands, now looking at Ms. Lin.

"I can have a faculty member take you, Nakoma." Ms. Lin said, motioning to Darlene to find someone.

"No, Ms. Lin! I trust Pete, and he already knows where I'm staying." Nakoma said knowing that it didn't sound right. Ms. Lin gave her a look of skepticism.

"He brought me pizza over the weekend. He delivers pizza. He knows where I'm staying." Now she sounded worse trying to backpedal out of the answers she was giving. Ms. Lin still looked at her, with question.

"Fine, I guess it would be okay." Ms. Lin said as she relaxed her composure and gave into sympathy for Nakoma. Nakoma made her way to study hall and found Pete.

"Come on, I need you to take me to town for something." Nakoma said, standing over Pete with a look of urgency.

"What about school?" Pete looked at her in confusion.

"I told the principle you were taking me home. So let's go!" She motioned with her head to the side. Pete sprang up from his seat, grabbing his stuff. He followed Nakoma out to his car. Once they got in, he took a deep breath.

"So where are we going?" Pete pulled his car keys out of his bag.

"To the salon. I'm donating my hair to Locks of Love." She said, putting on her seat belt.

"Oh! Good reason." Pete had s look of disappointment on his face.

"What, Pete?" Nakoma stared at him like *what's the problem?*

"It's just that I really like your hair, and…"

"Pete, I'm giving it to kids with cancer who need it more than I do. Anyways, do you know how much this weighs? It's a hassle. When we're done with that, there's something I need to show you." Pete started the car and drove off.

Pete and Nakoma made their way to the salon, where they met with Diana the hairdresser. She was smiling from ear to ear when Nakoma and Pete walked in.

"Nakoma! "I'm sorry to hear about your folks, honey. Shouldn't you be in school right now? Today's the day? Been waiting for you."

"Hi, Diana, thanks, Yes, today is the day." Nakoma smiled as she made her way to Diana.

"Then come sit down right here, honey. Let old Diana take that extra weight."

Nakoma just smiled as she made her way to the chair. Pete just stood at the door, looking totally out of place. Diana began to brush Nakoma's hair, putting bands in to hold it in place.

"Now, where do you want it cut at, honey?" She asked, looking at Nakoma in the mirror and smiling.

"At the shoulder, Diana. I still want to put it up if I can." Nakoma said, smiling back as she prepared for Diana to do her work.

"No problem honey, and you, young man, have a seat. You're blocking the doorway. Never know when a potential customer might walk in." Diana motioned to Pete with the scissors in her hand at him. But no one ever really did. Pete took a seat, still feeling awkward. Nakoma looked in the mirror. Diana made three quick cuts with the scissors. Nakoma could see Pete's expression of shock. It was done and the loss of weight felt good.

"There you go, honey. All done." Diana collected the hair into a bag labeled for St. Jude donations.

"Thanks Diana!" Nakoma got up, making her way to the door. Pete jumped up and followed.

"Thanks again, Diana!" She said as the two of them left the salon.

"No problem, honey, and the kids thank you too." Diana held up the bag in victory.

"Let's go to my family's farm. We can talk along the way." Nakoma got into Pete's car.

"Okay, Nakoma!" Pete said, as they got into the car and drove away from the salon. He was still shocked at what she had done. During the drive there, Nakoma told him the story of her being the Spirit Walker.

CHAPTER 16
NEW PLAYERS

Dr. **Underwood** was what would be called an obsessed man. His research in the theories of Nikola Tesla, had led him down a path of insanity or pure genius. Tesla's theories and projects ranged from the concepts of wireless communications, X-rays, and radio remote control. Dr. Underwood came to the path of science from his great-great grandfather who wrote articles about Nikola Tesla. Underwood, being obsessed, even went so far as to have Tesla's body exhumed for further research and analysis, hoping to possibly find an x-factor within him. He also studied Thomas Edison to see if he had stolen more than AC motors from Tesla. He did find it interesting when he learned just recently of two events: the fields being burnt in Kansas by lightning storms and a logging camp being destroyed in Washington state by lightning. Both were near Native lands. He studied Tesla so closely that he believed that he was also searching for the mighty Thunderbird during the period when he lived out west for a brief time. He had made several phone calls to reservations across the US, hoping that someone had some answers. Until today, he had gotten nowhere; then he left a message with Samuel Red Cloud, the leader of the Lakota nation.

"Sir, there's a message from a Dr. Underwood in New York. He wishes to meet with you." Samuel's secretary Barbera said, awaiting a response. Dr. Kim Baysinger's body lay dead on the floor.

"Dr. McFadden, what do you know of this Dr. Underwood?" Samuel turned at looked at her as he was wiping the blood from his knife with a towel.

"He's a crackpot, sir! The scientific community has barred him from being recognized in his field." She said, standing a little uneasily before Samuel.

"What is his field of study, doctor?" Samuel put the knife into the sheath on his back and walked over to the bar to pour himself a glass of scotch.

"He chases the theories of Nikola Tesla, studying how to control current and produce power. He does understand the coils better than I. But he's insane, sir! It would probably set us back on testing." She said, looking at the body on the floor.

"Excellent Dr. McFadden. Maybe a little crazy is what we need around here. Get him here tomorrow, and, here, wear this from now on. Samuel tossed her a leather strapped necklace with a pouch. I can't afford unexpected guests to arrive, and welcome to the team. Go see Lou, my security guard, for details."

"Yes, sir! Thank you, sir."

Dr. McFadden looked at the woman on the floor as she left the room, putting the necklace on. Samuel began to smile as he turned and looked out his window in his office, taking another drink of his scotch.

"Barbera, call the judge and tell him I want a restraining order on Tim Dobbson. I don't want him near the res. Tell him I'll give him a forty thousand marker at the casino for his trouble."

"Yes, Mr. Red Cloud!" Barbera said, rushing to get his request started.

"Oh! Call Detective Lane as well. I want an update on the reports."

"Yes, Mr. Red Cloud!"

"Soon, son, I will control this power of yours, and we can bring vengeance for all our Native lands. Taking back what is ours." Samuel looked now at a video monitor of his son in the cell.

"On second thought, Barbera patch me through to Underwood." Samuel stood at his desk ready to answer the phone.

The phone rang.

"Hello?"

"Dr. Underwood, Chief Red Cloud! You wanted to speak with me. How are you doing today, doctor?" Samuel asked then took a drink of his scotch.

"Good, good! I'm glad you returned my call, sir." Dr. Underwood was now smiling. Barbera walked back in, handing Samuel the flight reservation.

"I want you on the first flight tomorrow to Denver. It will leave there at 5:00 a.m. there in New York. Flight number 1257 out of Kennedy. You will be picked up by my associates George and Lou when you arrive. You can't miss them. They will bring you here to the reservation. Once you're here, we can discuss what would be expected of you." Samuel hung up the call and took another drink.

"Thank you, sir!" Dr. Underwood stood holding the phone to his ear for several minutes after the call. A smile appeared on his face. Then he began to jump around and frolic throughout his apartment. His apartment was cluttered with boxes and scattered research papers. He looked like a hoarder of junk to most. He finally snapped out of it a few moments later.

"Oh my! I must pack right away. What do I take? Toothbrush yes, toothpaste, my work. Oh dear, what does he seek?" *'The Thunderbird, you idiot, that is what he seeks.'* "Maybe he has it already!" *'The Thunderbird, no! Way too powerful to control. Maybe!'* "Maybe he wants to catch it!" *'Yes, yes, that's it! He wants us to help him catch it.'*

Dr. Underwood also suffered from multiple personalities, leading most in the scientific field to their conclusion of his insanity. Several hours passed as Dr. Underwood frantically moved around his apartment, going through his things, grabbing all he could and putting them into a briefcase.

"Sir, Dr. Underwood just received a phone call from a Samuel Red Cloud in Colorado. It has also been confirmed there is a plane ticket for him to go to Colorado tomorrow morning. What do you want us to do?" Agent Greene said, looking at his computer and, running the data of his surveillance.

"Agent Greene, he is your assignment. You and Folsome get there and follow him. We'll send in a sweep team to check the apartment tomorrow after he leaves. Maybe we missed something."

"Yes sir!' Greene was already reserving the jet to go to Colorado.

"Meet with the director there. Looks like the office in Colorado has been speaking to a Detective Lane involving an incident with Red Cloud already, but they have lost contact over the last few days. I'll call ahead to the Colorado office and let them know you two are coming."

"Yes Sir!" Agent Greene hung up the phone with his director. "The office in Colorado has spoken to Detective Lane. We will touch base with him when we get there."

"We've been sitting on this guy for two years, James. Every one of the Bureau thinks that Director Duncan is a crackpot with us along with him, period." Agent Greene said closing his lap-top and putting it into a backpack.

"It's a job, Dave, and it pays the same no matter what department we're in." Agent Folsome smiled at him, knowing what Greene said was true.

"Yeah but being labeled a ghost hunter or an X-Files reject won't get us promoted." Agent Greene put the backpack onto the back seat behind him.

"No, it will not, but you can always put in for a transfer. Maybe you'll get the tax evasion of Donald Trump. That's good, I hear." Agent Folsome said, smiling as he started the vehicle.

"All I know right now is that we've got new players on the field. By the look of it, we're looking at some supernatural shit, James." Agent Greene said, rolling down his window in the passenger seat and lighting a cigarette.

"You mean you're not going to consider a desk job, checking on politicians and climate control reviews?"

Folsome smiled as he pulled into traffic heading toward the airport.

"Asshole! You know what I'm saying. If this is a ghost hunt, our careers are over." Agent Greene said in frustration, flicking half of his cigarette out the window.

"Easy, partner. We all do our part, if we do what's right. Then we do it with the integrity and honor. Most of all, we're not cops. We investigate and report. The way I see it, things just got more fun." Agent Folsome just smiled as he came to a stop at an intersection.

"You're right, James, but this feels like a rabbit hole I'm not ready for." Agent Greene replied as he pulled a pack of gum from his jacket pocket.

"David, you can't give back the red pill now. You're in the matrix. He's our little white rabbit, so let's go and do our job." Agent Folsome began to chuckle. Agent Greene put a piece of gum in his mouth, looking at James and chuckling along with him.

CHAPTER 17

MAGNITUDE

Pete and Nakoma made it to her family's home. Pulling up, Pete could see the destruction.

"Wow, Nakoma. This is bad!" Pete said, still looking at the rubble of what was once her home.

"I know, Pete. There have to be some clues here." Nakoma said as Pete stopped his car.

"The police and fire have already been here, and Tim. If there were any clues, wouldn't they have found them already?" Pete placed the car in park and turned off the engine.

"Haven't you been listening, Pete? They were murdered. Red Cloud owns the police, and who knows, whoever else. But I have some ways of my own to see the truth." Nakoma got out of the car, and Pete followed suit.

"What do you mean?" Pete replied, still not knowing if her story was made up.

"Red Cloud's son is the Thunderbird. Me and Debbie found out. Red Cloud is keeping it a secret and tying up loose ends." Nakoma stopped and turned to look at Pete.

"So, you're a loose end?" Pete was now starting to put the pieces together in his mind, and worry crossed his face.

"Yes, Pete, and now so are you. I'm sorry that I brought you into this, but I need your help in finding Jeromia. His father is a bad man. I know he wants to use Jeromia and his new power to. Well, it's bad Pete."

Nakoma turned and looked toward the barn, she could see the back end of Tim's truck. She rushed over with Pete close behind. As she approached, she could see Tim slouched over the steering wheel. Her heart raced as she ran to the truck.

"Tim!" Nakoma cried out, running with tears in her eyes. Tim woke, looking up at Nakoma running toward him.

Tony smacked Frank as he looked upon Nakoma and Pete running to the truck.

"Nakoma! What are you doing here, kid?" Tim saw the tears in her eyes as she ran up. Nakoma stopped short of the truck, still crying and, realizing Tim was okay. Tim got out of the truck and gave her a hug as Pete stood in awkward silence and kicked a few rocks.

"Oh now, kid. I'm fine. I just missed them too. And none of this makes any sense. I've gone over the reports and the property here, but it doesn't add up." Tim said, looking back toward the house.

"It's Red Cloud, Tim. He's after me, and I have to stop him." Nakoma wiped the tears from her eyes.

"Oh, now kid that's crazy. How do you know that?" Tim looked at her, not understanding what she was saying.

"I have to show you, but I didn't mean for any of this to happen. Pete, you too." Nakoma stepped back from them.

"Show us what, Nakoma?" Tim now was concerned that she did know something.

Nakoma took the bracelet off, turning it into the headdress. Tim and Pete jumped back in surprise. She placed it on her head, and, instantly, she was the Spirit Walker. Her eyes glowed for a minute, and then she blinked, letting her brown eyes show.

Tim and Pete stepped back a few more feet, freaked out about what just happened.

"Whoa, Nakoma. What is this?" Tim looked at her in disbelief.

"I've been chosen to be the Spirit Walker, and Red Cloud's son is the Thunderbird." Nakoma said standing before them.

"Awesome!" Pete said, now smiling from ear to ear and jumping in the air.

"What... your voice, your eyes were like blue fire..." Tim was unsettled by what was happening.

"I stopped his son from killing someone and brought him back to the motel where me Debbie and I was staying. We put him in a taxi to go back to his dorm room. They tracked us here, Tim, killing my parents and Debbie. I've put you all in danger." Then Nakoma's attention was drawn to the hillside.

"We're being watched. Stay here." Nakoma vanished before their eyes.

"Where did she go, Frank?" As Tony sat up in the truck, looking to where Nakoma went.

"I don't..." Just then, Nakoma appeared at Frank's door. ripping the door off the truck and grabbing Frank. Nakoma dropped the door and removed him from his seat, holding him high in the air by his throat.

"Useless!" Nakoma said, tossing Frank like a rag doll about thirty feet away behind her. Tony pulled his gun, aiming it at Nakoma as she vanished only to appear at his door. Nakoma tore his door off, grabbing him by the gun arm and pulling him out of the truck. Fear shook Tony so intently he wet himself. Nakoma threw the door to the side, now looking at Tony.

"Where is Jeromia?" Nakoma said, slamming him to the ground by his arm. Tony was in total fear as he dropped the gun.

"New warehouse out by Tiffany. That's where Red Cloud is keeping Him. Please don't kill me. We're just watching and reporting." Tony cried, hoping that he would not die.

"Then report this: I'm coming!" Nakoma picked up Tony. With one hand, she slammed him into the side of the bed of the truck. She let him go and vanished before him. Nakoma then appeared in front of Tim and Pete.

"Holy shit!" Tim said, looking at Nakoma. Pete was still smiling from ear to ear and dancing around.

"You're not safe, Tim. I must go for a while. I have to find Jeromia." Nakoma looked at him with sadness.

"This is awesome!" Pete blurted out with excitement.

"That goes for you too Pete. Stay away from all this." As she turned toward Pete.

"But you said you needed my help. I thought we were going to be- a team like Batman and Robin."

Nakoma removed her headdress, changing back into her normal self. She Looked at the headdress.

"I was wrong!" She walked over to Pete, placing her hand on his shoulder.

"What do you want us to do, Nakoma? If they already know who we are..." Tim said, now worrying.

"Nothing! He wants to tie up loose ends. Well, this loose end is coming for him." Nakoma said, turning back toward Tim. He could see the anger in her eyes.

"What is going on, Nakoma?" Tim took a step toward her.

"She's the Spirit Walker, guardian of the spirit world protecting the earth." Pete rambled in excitement.

"Pete!" Nakoma turned back around to him with a look of seriousness.

"Oh sorry, Nakoma, I mean, Spirit Walker." Pete motioned with hand as if to zip his lip. "Yes."

"Pete, you seem to know enough. Can you follow Tim home, and then fill him in? Tim, you're all I have left, so please be careful." Nakoma said, as she turned back toward him.

"I just can't make a sense of this." Tim stood looking at her.

"Pete will inform you of what you need to know for now. I have to find Red Cloud, period." Nakoma put the head dress back on and vanished. The sound of Tony's shitty truck was heard leaving the hillside, moving away from the farm.

"Let's go, Pete, before someone else shows up." Tim got back in his truck.

"Side-kick, I'm a side kick. I'll follow you." Pete ran to his car. The two left the area, heading back to Tim's trailer.

Nakoma sat in the spirit world fixed on Tony. She focused on the area he went to. He was not lying as he approached the gated area with a warehouse. The two guards at the gate radioed head for confirmation. Then they allowed the truck to pass through. Once they were there at the warehouse, they were met by George and Lou. Frank and Tony were patted down and then escorted into the building. Instantly, Nakoma felt pain as Tony got inside. It was as if a huge migraine headache hit her, and Tony felt it too. Nakoma maintained her focus, watching as the four men came before the cage in the room. Frank and Tony were unsettled by the sight. Samuel approached and met them at the cage.

"I thought I was clear." Samuel said drawing their attention away from George and Lou who were now standing behind them.

"Yes, sir. But the girl is powerful, and she found us." Tony said, now scared of the look the Samuel was giving him.

"She ripped me out of the truck and then threw me." Frank said anger. Lou stabbed Frank in the back, and Frank fell to the ground choking on his own blood. Blood ran from his lips as he collapsed on the floor.

"I'm sorry, Mr. Red Cloud. Please don't kill me." Tony pleaded for his life.

"Funny. It's an oversight I made with you. Isn't it Spirit Walker? I know you're in there, seeing and listening to us." Samuel now realized that she had used the two men to see where he was.

"What?" Tony looked confused as his body shook in fear.

"You see, Mr. Arjun, I wear this pouch of warding, like many of my associates. It keeps the spirits away. You don't have any wards or one of these pouches. Which in turn by letting you go, she used you to see me. This is most unfortunate for you, Mr. Arjun." Samuel now turned away from him. George and Lou grabbed Tony, and he began to squirm.

"Wait, wait, Mr. Red Cloud, please." Tony cried in his plead. Samuel walked up to Tony's left ear. Looking at his son in the cage.

"Shh, Mr. Arjun. Now listen, Spirit Walker. I have the Thunderbird and will use him to take back what is ours. Freeing our people, our lands, taking back everything the white man stole." Samuel saw Jeromia stand, overhearing the conversation. Samuel smiled as he backed away from Tony.

"So, stay out of my way, Nakoma Standing Elk. Or everything else you love will end." As soon as Samuel said Nakoma's name, Jeromia became enraged, turning into the Thunderbird and screaming as lightning filled the cage. The whole warehouse shook from its thunder.

"Interesting. You know this girl?" Samuel replied walking toward his son. "Oh, don't worry, son. I'll have her power too."

The Thunderbird became more enraged, charging up with so much power that it looked like light covered the entire room, he was in, blinding everyone in the room. Then the Thunderbird slammed his fist into the floor. The lightning went into the coils routing to the rod in the center, and the thunder was so devastating that it caused an earthquake, bringing the whole warehouse down around everyone. Nakoma's link was broken. One of the steel beams came down and crushed Tony, killing him instantly. George and Lou covered Samuel on the ground as debris fell all around. Nakoma screamed from the pain of Tony's death, and fear consumed her as she did not know if Jeromia was okay.

Tim and Pete had just returned to the trailer as the earthquake hit. The quake hit so hard that the trailer fell off its stands, causing the water and gas lines to break. Windows shattered, as they dropped to the floor, and car alarms rang out throughout the trailer park.

"Are you okay, Pete?" Tim said, trying to get to his feet.

"Yeah, I think so. What was that?" Pete sat on the ground a moment looking at the things that fell inside.

"Earthquake, a big one." Tim got to his feet and help Pete up. "Call your folks. See if they're okay."

"Yeah, I will." Pete pulled out his phone and called home.

"Come on, Nakoma pick up." Tim called Nakoma, but there was no answer. "Damn it."

"Mom is everything okay? Yes, I'm fine. Yes, Mom, I'm coming home right now. I got to go, Tim." Pete brushed himself off.

"Okay, son, be careful. We'll talk later. I got to get these lines turned off and go to the firehouse." Tim said, making his way to the back to grab his toolbox.

"Yes, sir, I will." Pete looked around the trailer again in shock.

"Thanks, Pete! Nakoma is lucky to have you as her friend right now." Tim went out back, and Pete just smirked, thinking 'Sidekick to the Spirit Walker. This is the coolest thing ever.'

It took about an hour for Tim to get the gas and water lines shut off. He then left to go the station to see what efforts were being made to help the community.

CHAPTER 18

BEHIND BARRIERS

Nakoma returned to Tim's trailer in her room. She saw, realizing the destruction of the quake, Tim was not there. She focused her attention on him, seeing that he was helping with search and rescue efforts for the town. She turned her attention to Pete, and he was helping his parents at home. Knowing that they were safe, she focused on principal Lin at the school. Principal Lin was hurt and pinned inside her office. Nakoma appeared before her. Principal Lin was hit with fear when she saw Nakoma appear.

"It's okay Principal Lin I'm here to help." Nakoma said in her ghostly voice, her eyes looking like blue fire.

"Nakoma!" Ms. Lin said as she passed out from shock. Then Nakoma saw a tree outside the window. She asked the tree for help. The tree began to lean toward the window, reaching its heavy branches through, grabbing the stone pieces around Principal Lin. The stone was too heavy for the tree to move, and it almost made things worse.

"Wait! I'll have to try something else." Nakoma said as she watched the tree go back to its regular form. Looking at Lin, she leaned down, touching Ms. Lin's hand

and thinking of Tim. Instantly her and Lin were in front of him on the ground.

"Shit, Nakoma!" Tim jumped in shock and fear.

"She needs your help." Nakoma vanished again.

"Well, Roscoe, get the triage station set up. We'll have incoming." Tim said, rushing to Ms. Lin to help her with her injuries.

Over the next few hours, Nakoma had brought thirty-six people to the aid station. She was exhausted. Tim could see the toll that it took on her.

"Hey, wait! You need to rest." Tim said, trying to get her to stop.

"I can't. People need me." She replied, placing her hands on her knees.

"You've done good for now. We can handle the rest from here, Nakoma." Just then Nakoma was bumped and shooed away by GES.

"Shoo now, girl. You need rest!" She used a towel to wave at Nakoma to get away. Nakoma just nodded and vanished before their eyes. Tim turned around to tell GES an explanation of what just happened, but she was gone too. He stood there scratching his head.

"Come on, Mr. Red Cloud, let's get you out of here." George said, helping him up as Lou held a piece of debris up for them to get through.

"Check on the cage and find Dr. McFadden." Samuel said as the two men cleared the way.

Screams of pain could be heard, as several of the scientists were injured. Lou made his way to the control rooms and found Dr. McFadden, under her desk shaking with fear. He was able to clear a path to her. Several of her colleagues were either dead or badly hurt.

"Come now doctor, this way." Lou said as he motioned with his hand for her to come on. Dr. McFadden came out and she could see the destruction around her.

"Help me!" One scientist moaned in pain. She stopped to look back.

"Come on, doctor." Lou said again, ignoring the other victims. Samuel and George made their way to the cage, looking to see if it was still intact.

"Damn! The whole thing is done. Get the restraints out of the van. We'll have to move to the sacred circle." Samuel said pounding his fist on a piece of the cage.

Jeromia lie unconscious in the center from the blast. He had created a crater as big as the cage itself and several feet deep. Security teams we're now entering the building to help the wounded.

"No witnesses. I also need you in Denver tomorrow to pick up Dr. Underwood. Take the limo." Samuel said, now turning to exit the warehouse.

"Yes, Mr. Red Cloud." George said, signaling to the guards with the gesture of slitting throats. The guards opened fire on the wounded and already dead. Moments later, there was silence. Samuel made his way out of the warehouse to this car and drove away.

"What was that?" Seismologist Jenni Kern asked. looking at the seismographs.

"That's impossible. These waves came from southern Colorado, and there are no lines there. Did we just get nuked?" Jenni picked up the phone and called Tom Holland, her director.

"Hey, Tom, these waves came from southern Colorado. Are we under attack or something?" Jenni said trying to figure out what just happened.

"No, Ms. Kern, we are not. Get down there and find out what happened." Tom said as he put down his beer on the table on his back porch and took a drag off a cigar.

"Yes, sir!" Jenni said, scrambling to get things ready to go.

"By the book, Jenni! That's reservation territory, and you're an outsider." Tom leaned forward in his seat, rolling the ashes of his cigar into an ashtray.

"Yes, Tom, by the book. I'll call when I have some news." Jenni hung up the phone, scrambling to get her equipment to the van.

"Dr. McFadden, go to the van and help open the doors." Lou said as he and George were putting restraints on Jeromia.

"Chief wants him at the sacred circle. Help me get him out." George said, lifting Jeromia's limp body. Lou proceeded to help George take Jeromia to the van where Dr. McFadden was waiting.

"Did you not just see what happened in there? We can't control this. We must stop now. I'm not doing this anymore." Dr. McFadden expressed. Georgia and Lou placed Jeromia in the back of the van. As Dr. McFadden, leaned in to look to see if he was okay. Lou pulled a syringe from his pocket. He hit Dr. McFadden with it in the back of the neck, knocking her out with the sedative. She collapsed part way into the van. Then Lou placed her body fully into the back of the van with Jeromia. George and Lou got into the front seats, and they drove off heading to the sacred circle.

Nakoma appeared before the great tree in the spirit world, making her way to the pool. GES appeared in front of her holding Bob.

"Are Tim and Pete, okay?" Nakoma asked in her determined walk.

"They're fine dear." GES said with a sad look on her face.

Nakoma petted Bob as she continued past to the pool. GES followed beside her. Once Nakoma reached the pool, the stones rose to make a path to the center. Nakoma made her way to the center, now driven to find answers.

"Warriors of the past, those who have fought the Thunderbird, come forth and aid me now." Nakoma said, standing firm as two light orbs approached and took form. They were both females as they took shape. One was Navajo by the attire she wore, and the other was Aztec in appearance. Both were beautiful and strong as they now stood before her.

"How do I find him?" Nakoma asked looking at each of them. The two spirits just stood looking at her.

"How do I see through what is blocking me?" She asked, trying to find an answer.

"You cannot!" The Navajo spirit said.

"The wards used are to protect the mortal world from the spirit world." The Aztec spirit said.

"Now that the Thunderbird has destroyed his cage he will be moved to a sacred place." The Navajo spirit said.

"The truth is in the stone you wear. It is used for good and evil." The Aztec spirit said

"How do I stop him when I find him?" Both spirits placed their hands over their hearts and turned back into orbs of light. "Then aid me now!" Nakoma commanded.

The two orbs flew into stone of her bone collar adding two more beads. Her outfit changed to a pair of hide leather pants and a top that was cut at the mid drift, and a shield appeared on her back. It was heavy, lined with copper, and a copper spear appeared in her right hand. She could feel the presence of the other two Spirit Walkers. Nakoma then vanished back to her room at Tim's trailer. She took the headdress off, turning it back into a bracelet and placing it upon her wrist. She cleared off an area of the bed and laid down to sleep. GES appeared with Bob and laid him on the bed.

'Thanks, GES!" Nakoma said as Bob lie beside her, purring away.

"Rest now, dear. Tomorrow's another day." GES said with a loving smile, then vanished Nakoma fell asleep.

CHAPTER 19

INVESTIGATION

Agents Greene and Folsome landed in Denver the next morning, several hours ahead of Dr. Underwood. They had already contacted the office there in Denver, to let them know that they were there and that they would be waiting on Dr. Underwood to arrive at the airport. Three hours later, Flight 1257 landed. When Dr. Underwood left the airplane, he made his way to the exit, where he was met by George and Lou.

"James, those boys are big!" Agent Greene said in shock.

"Yeah, those tax reports on the president are looking a lot better right now." Agent Folsome replied, checking to make sure his gun was still there. Agent Greene took pictures of the two men with his phone. George was holding up a sign for Mr. Underwood. People passing by walked away from their presence.

"I'm Dr. Underwood!" Dr. Underwood shouted through the crowd as he held up his hand, waving it like a child in a school-room class.

"Put this on." George said as he motioned with his head to Lou. Then Lou handed him a necklace with a pouch.

"What is it for?" Dr. Underwood asked, taking it form Lou's hand and looking at it strangely.

"So, you don't get hurt on the res." Lou said walking to position himself behind the doctor.

"Okay." Dr. Underwood put the necklace on, following George and Lou out to a limousine, and they drove away. Greene and Folsome made their way out of the airport after the three men had left, making their way to the FBI office in Denver.

Ms. Kern was standing at the front desk after have traveled, several hours from Golden, Colorado, to the FBI office there in Denver. She was there when Greene and Folsome walked in.

"Excuse me, gentlemen, do you guys work here?" Jenni said trying to get their attention.

"I'm Agent Greene, and this is Agent Folsome. We work in the FBI yes." Agent Greene looked at her with a stone wall look.

"I need to get into the reservation to check the unknown quake yesterday, and I was hoping you could lend me some assistance or point me to someone who can help." Jenni said now noticing that Agent Folsome was checking her out.

"We're not a part of this office." Agent Greene said as he and Folsome walked by her.

"But we do have business on the reservation ourselves and seeing Mrs. Kern works for a federal agency as well." Folsome said as Greene elbowed him in the side.

"We're sorry, Mrs. Kern. You would have to check with the reservation yourself on those matters." Agent Greene said, continuing on to the back of the building.

"Ms. Kern. I'm not married." Jenni said to clarify the introduction.

"I'm James. Here's my card. Maybe if something else comes up, we can catch a drink." Folsome said, giving her a wink.

"Maybe I could tag along." Jenni asked, taking the card from Agent Folsome.

"No, Ms. Kern. I doubt our investigations are related. You'll have to check with the reservation." Greene said as he stopped to look at her.

Folsom whispered to her. "Call me." Giving her his charming smile and another wink.

As the two men went further into the office, Ms. Kern stood frustrated, placing the business card in her backpack.

"Fine. Don't blame me when the investigation leads back to me, Agent Greene!" Ms. Kern said, leaving the office.

"She's hot right?" Folsom said, following Greene. checking his breath and hoping he didn't blow it.

"Yes, she is pretty, James" Greene replied.

The two agents made their way to Director Jennings's office and knocked on the door.

"Come in."

"Sir, Director Duncan sent us to follow Dr. Underwood." Greene said, standing before Director Jennings's desk.

"Yes, he called. Come in and have a seat." Director Jennings motioned with his hand to the two seats in front of his desk.

"Do you know these two men?" Greene said, holding up his phone with the picture of George and Lou.

"Personal bodyguards of Chief Red Cloud. They do all his dirty work." Jennings said, picking up a binder off his desk.

"Who's Chief Red Cloud?" Folsome asked as he took his seat and adjusted his suite jacket.

"Head of the Lakota tribe in the Dakotas, and apparently here on the Ute reservation down south." Jennings said, now standing up.

"What's he doing here?" Greene asked, sitting back in his seat.

"From what we know he's an artifact and art dealer. He just had an exhibit at Colorado University this last weekend. He has set up residence on the reservation. As to what we do know. The quake yesterday came from the reservation, not to mention the explosion at the Grand Hotel that happened in the penthouse where he was staying. I need you two to get into contact with Detective Lane. He's refusing to answer our calls. There's car a waiting in the garage, A2. Here's a file on Lane." Jennings said, handing Greene the file.

"Director, we're supposed to follow Underwood." Folsome said, leaning forward in his chair.

"Find Lane, learn what he knows." Jennings sat back down in his chair.

"Yes, sir." Agent Greene said, as the two got up and headed out.

"This is getting very weird, Dave." Folsome said once out-side the director's door scratching his head trying to figure out what was next.

"Well at least we know we're Underwood is at." Greene said passing, the file back to Folsome.

"Yeah, but this just got interesting. Crazy scientist, now a chief of Native American tribe." Folsome was beginning to feel like the agent he was when he was a rookie eager and energetic, ready to take on the world.

"Come on, we'll get something to eat before we go find Lane." Greene said as he made his way to the front.

Agent Folsome was close behind. "Do you think she'll call?" He asked Greene as he tucked the file under his left arm, following him out.

"Yeah, sure, and in ten years, you'll be on your third failed marriage, wondering if you should just eat a bullet or find a fourth wife." Greene said, trying to shut James up.

Fact of the matter was that David had previously married twice before. With three kids and alimony, he was barely able to survive as it was. He had spent the last three years burying himself in his work. James had only known David for a short time as he had only been assigned to be his partner four months ago. James was young at the age of twenty-seven and had only been with the agency for two years now. David had ten years in, and it was obvious he lacked the youthfulness of James. He did know that being a federal agent was hard and having a family life just didn't fit into the equation for him. James on the other hand was still caught up in serving his country. He was a looker, too at six-two and two hundred pounds, with light brown skin and a perfect fade haircut, tying it all up with soft brown eyes. He would give Will Smith a run for his money.

David was six feet tall with a black receding hairline in the front. He weighed around 215 pounds with a solid build. His green eyes could pierce anyone into a guilty plea. He was jaded when he spoke most of the time, always seeming to be the serious one of the partnership.

"I get it, man, but it wouldn't kill you lighten up a little." James said as he followed him to the parking garage.

CHAPTER 20

SEARCHING FOR LANE

Agents Greene and Folsome went to the Denver Police Department to talk to Detective Lane. They approached the desk sergeant and requested to see him.

"How can I help you boys?" Sergeant Shirley Miller asked. Shirley was one of the older officers of the department. She had spent her earlier years working parking enforcement, but she carried herself well and was loved and respected by her coworkers.

Agent Greene flashed his badge. "We would like to speak to Detective Lane."

"He's not here, sugar." Shirley said, now looking at Folsome.

"Do you know where we can find him, ma'am?" Agent Folsome said, trying to add charm with a smile.

"Well, he doesn't come in much, but he does have a set routine every day. Is he in trouble?" Shirley sat up straighter in her chair.

"No, ma'am, we're just looking for some information on a case he might be able to help us with." Folsome said, leaning on her desk and still smiling, hoping that she would spill the beans of his whereabouts.

"I should hopefully hope not. He's our best detective. At around nine, he gets his coffee down on Third Street. Wednesdays, he goes to Subway for lunch. Down on Jefferson around 11. But most of the department catches their cool off time at O'Leary's on Frankfurt. You can usually catch him there at the end of the bar." Shirley said, reaching over to touch Folsome's hand in the banter between them.

"Thank you, ma'am." Agent Greene said, tapping Folsome on the arm to go. Folsome picked up her hand and kissed it like any gentleman would do meeting a lady in the eighteenth century, pouring on the Chivalry as he stood to leave.

"No problem. You boys be safe out there."

"Yes, ma'am. Thank you." Folsome said, smiling as he turned to follow Greene out. Greene and Folsome got into their car.

"Well," Folsom said as the two walked out of the station.

"O'Leary's, it is long shot right now, but we can probably wait till he shows." Greene replied.

The two men drove to O'Leary's pub and went in. As they went in there were several people seated at tables. The room was dark but lit with a low light. They noticed a man at the end of the bar hunched over a drink. The bartender waved hello and gave a nod as he continued to clean the glasses.

"Watch the door, Folsome. I'll talk to him." Greene made his way to the man and sat next to him.

"What can I get you, sir?" The bartender asked placing a napkin in front of Agent Greene.

"Club soda!" Greene opened his badge and placed it on the bar. "I'm looking for Lane."

Lane looked up at him putting his finger over his lips to be quiet and pulled a notepad and pen from his jacket and wrote <u>Sherly told you</u>. He passed the notepad to Agent Greene.

Agent Greene wrote: "*Yes, we need your help with Chief Red Cloud information*" He passed the notepad back.

"*I can't. He put a tracker in my neck with an explosive charge. If I talk or go where I'm not supposed to. He'll kill me. He's connected deep.*" Lane wrote then passed the notepad back. Greene nodded in understanding.

Detective Lane paused, and then reached into his jacket and handed him a flash drive under a napkin on the bar that said *Help*. Greene took the napkin and flash drive. He then laid fifty dollars on the bar.

"Thanks. Have a good night." Greene got up and headed out with Folsome close behind. They got back into the car.

"Well, what did he say?" Folsome asked as he was putting on his seat belt.

"Red Cloud is our target. We have to be careful who we talk to. Secure the laptop information and plug this in. We're going to the reservation tomorrow." Agent Greene said as he started the car.

"What did he say?" Folsome had never seen this side of David. He was now driven, more or less pissed off.

"He has a slave chip in his neck that Red Cloud controls. He's been..." David gripped the steering wheel. He hated the ugly truth that officers could be bought or manipulated, by someone with a little power.

"He's been compromised" Folsome said, looking at David, now realizing things were going to get bad really soon.

Agent Greene nodded as he put the car in drive. The two men drove toward the reservation. That evening, they caught up with the Bayfield police chief, Ryan Givens, outside the disaster relief tents at the football field.

CHAPTER 21

MS. KERN

George and Lou drove to the reservation, escorting Dr. Underwood to Red Cloud's residence. About three hours into the drive, they stopped for gas. Dr. Underwood had to use the bathroom.

He was in there for almost an hour. Lou became agitated trying to hurry him up as he banged upon the door. He then came out, and Lou gave him a stern look.

"I'm sorry. It's been over eight hours, and I don't like flying." Underwood said shying away from Lou.

It was obvious that Dr. Underwood didn't feel comfortable around the two men as Lou escorted him back to the limo. George had finished filling up the limo and got back in, and they drove away. Three more hours later, they arrived at Red Cloud's home.

Ms. Kern spent the night in Denver that night at a local motel, and in the morning, she got up and drove to the reservation. Six hours later, she had finally made her way to Bayfield, Colorado. There she saw the destruction of the quake. As she drove through, she saw the police and fire station building in ruins. Then she saw tents on the high school football field. She pulled into the school.

"Well, Tim, GHSC is finally here." The fire chief, Corey Moore, said. Just then, Tim saw her get out of the truck. His mouth was wide open.

"Damn, Tim. Close your mouth or the possums will get you. She's all yours, buddy." Moore said, laughing at Tim.

"Hello, I'm Jenni Kern with the Geological Hazards Science Center in Golden, Colorado. Can you tell me what happened?" Tim just stood for a moment looking at her, as she held out her hand.

"Sorry, Tim Dobbson, deputy chief here in Bayfield. We're still waiting for FEMA to set up. But from what we can tell, it was a quake." He was surprised that her handshake was firm and that her skin felt so soft compared to his.

"Any news from the reservation on its location?" Jenni asked looking at the setup on the field.

"No, but response teams have been able to bring folks here for treatment." Tim said as he continued to look at her. He had never felt these feelings since his wife... Butterflies in his stomach fluttered as he stopped to take a deep breath.

"I need to get onto the reservation, and check its origin. Know anyone who can get me in." Jenni asked now focusing on Tim.

"Yes... I can take you. I'm half UTE, and I can take you on to the Res." Tim was totally taken by her as he looked into her eyes.

"When can we go?" Jenni smiled, for she liked that she was noticed. She did find him handsome, though she never thought of anything but her work in her life.

"Let me get with Chief and we can go." Tim smiled at her and then ran to the fire chief.

"Thanks, Tim." Jenni continued to smile with the feelings of child's joy inside. Moments later, they were in his truck headed for the reservation.

"Oh, I need to call Nakoma. Hang on." Tim said, reaching for his phone.

"Is that your wife?" Jenni asked as her thoughts turned to disappointment.

"No, my goddaughter. Her parents died, and she lives with me now." Tim replied as he dialed her number.

"I'm sorry." Jenni felt she had intruded now and felt foolish.

'Don't be. She's strong." Tim just smiled at her as Jenni showed concern. She could since Tim was a good man.

"So, you and your wife have children?" Jenni asked trying to get to know him.

"No, I'm not married. Well, I'm widowed. My wife and son died, about eight years ago. Bayfield is small. Not much of dating pool, you might say. Most women don't stick around for a small-town life." Tim seemed to jest, but it was hard and somewhat good to open up.

"I didn't mean to pry." Jenni now felt bad for asking as she looked at his face.

"No worries. There's enough here to keep me busy. And I like it here. How long are you staying?" Now Tim was wondering as he looked back at her.

"Just until I find the source of the quake, and I file my report." Jenni turned to look out the passenger window, thinking it wouldn't work between them.

"Well, maybe we can have dinner afterward. If you have time." He replied, hoping she would accept.

"That would be nice if I had the time." Jenni turned to face him again with a smile. Tim smiled back. Jenni looked at her map once they reached the reservation, pointing to the origin of the quack.

"It's here on the map." Jenni positioned the map so Tim could see.

"Yes, I know where that is." Tim said nodding his head.

"That's the point of the hypo center." Jenni said, now getting into her field of work.

"Hypo center?" Tim was confused, and Jenni smiled.

"Point of origin, Tim." Jenni smiled, forgetting Tim had no idea of the technical terms used to describe earth quakes. Thirty minutes later, they arrived at an abandoned facility.

"How is this possible? Nothing should be standing." Jenni said knowing the quake that was recorded should have leveled everything.

"I never knew the building was here." Tim was confused now, never knowing this place was even there. He had lived in Bayfield his whole life and didn't know of any of this construction. Tim and Jenni pulled up to the building. They both sat there looking at the collapsed warehouse.

"It's inside that building Tim." Jenni said, now eager to see as she hopped out of the truck.

"Wait!" Tim got out, quickly following. "I don't know if we should be here.

"It looks abandoned to me." She went in and Tim followed. They made their way to the destroyed cage.

"What is this? What are these symbols? What happened? The crater in the center is like a bomb went off. Those offices there is like they were observing something. This is no earthquake. What was in here?" Jenni looked in astonishment as she made her way around the debris.

"It's a cage and these symbols are ancient wards to trap or hold something powerful." Tim was aware of the ancient runes displayed. He was now very nervous.

"Ward's, like a monster?" Jenni looked at Tim with confusion on her face.

"Native beliefs across these lands still believe to be true. If I'm reading this right." Just then the Nakoma appeared behind him.

"It is the Thunderbird!" Tim and Jenni turned around, startled.

"What are you doing here, Nakoma?" Tim blurted out, scared of the whole situation.

"This is your goddaughter?' Jennie said in shock of seeing her.

"I need you to stay away from this, Tim, and not get anyone else involved." Nakoma said making her way to Tim and Jenni.

"Yes, Nakoma. What is Red Cloud doing?" Tim now didn't really want to know.

"He has moved Jeromia, but I cannot see. I came to look for clues once I saw you were here. These wards block my sight. I have to find Jeromia." Nakoma said in her ghostly voice. Tim bowed his head and thought, then looked at Nakoma

"Sacred circle. The only place he could." He replied, and Nakoma vanished before them. Jenni stood there in shock.

"Come, Jenni. Let's get off the res. and do what she asked." Jenni followed Tim to the truck, and they drove back to town.

"Where looking for the police chief." Folsome told one of the ladies helping some people get settled for the evening. The women pointed toward a trailer parked in the end zone on the west end. The two men went to the trailer and knocked. The police chief answered the door.

"Evening, sir, I'm Agent Greene and this is Agent Folsome." Greene showed his badge. "We're doing an investigation on a Samuel Red Cloud and was wondering if you know someone who can get us on the Reservation." Just then, Fire Chief Moore interrupted as he walked up.

"Tim Dobbson, my deputy fire chief, can help you. He's half Ute native." Moore said, looking at the two men as they turned around.

"Where can we find him, sir?" Folsome said as he reached to shake his hand.

He's with a lady from the GHSC Mrs. Kern, I believe."

"Ms. Kern. She's not married" Folsome replied with a smile. "Any ideas where they might be?"

"By now, they're probably having dinner over at Antonio's diner. It's just up the road there by the Walmart parking lot." Moore said, thinking Tim's evening was about to get ruined. Then he chuckled and walked away.

"We'll thank you, gentlemen" Greene said as they walked back toward the car.

"She's resourceful, to say the least." Folsome said as they got into the car.

"Yep, probably saved you a bad marriage by finding him." David said with a chuckle as he started the car and drove off.

"Not the lightening up I was suggesting, partner. That kinda hurts." James had to laugh with him on that jab to his ego.

CHAPTER 22

DINNER

That night, Tim told her the story over dinner at Antonio's diner. It was probably the largest restaurant in the town, and the quake hadn't affected it very much. The place was packed because people needed a place to eat. A lot of homes had been destroyed, and the ones who could afford to eat out did so at Antonio's. They sat in the back corner with a table for four and were pretty much lost in conversation.

"How do I report this? Who would believe me?" Jenni sat looking at Tim, pondering all that was said. Just then Agent Greene and Folsome came into the diner.

"Evening gentlemen. There's room at the bar if you would like, or you'd like to table..." The hostess was cut short.

"We're looking for the Deputy Chief Tim Dobbson." Greene said as he flashed his badge.

"He's over there with the scientist." The hostess replied, pointing to the back corner table. They looked over and saw Ms. Kern with Tim, and they made their way to them.

"Deputy Chief, Ms. Kern, may we join you?"

Agent Folsome asked flashing his badge with Greene, and both men sat down. For the next hour and a half, Tim shared his story with the three of them and everything he knew, with the exception of Nakoma's involvement.

"So, what am I supposed to tell my director at the GHSC? That a Native American god did this?" Jenni asked now looking at the two agents.

"No, Ms. Kern. We will notify your agency of a government exercise gone wrong and apologize for the late notification. It is best you go home tomorrow. Deputy Chief, can you take us to the reservation tomorrow, so we can see for ourselves?" Greene asked, looking at Tim.

"I was told to stay away." Tim became unsettled with his request.

"By whom? Red Cloud?" Folsome said with sarcasm in his voice.

"No, a spirit. If Red Cloud found me, I'd be dead already. You don't believe me or her, do you?" Tim became insulted with Folsome's remark.

"I will say things are a bit strange, but these are not the first. We just want to see for ourselves." Greene said, trying to calm the situation.

"The spirit said stay away. I'll show you on the map, but I'm not going." Tim gestured to Jenni to give him the map.

"Fair enough." Greene said as he looked at the map with Tim. "The food was good. Dinner is on us, and thanks for the help." The two men got up. Folsome laid two hundred dollars on the table, Agent Greene took Jenni's map, and the two men left.

"You're going too, aren't you?" Tim said, knowing Jenni was going to leave.

"I can't file my report till tomorrow with my director, but there are no rooms available in town, what with the quake and all." Jenni replied, looking at Tim with a smile.

"Just stay at my place if you like." He said, hoping she'd say yes, and the butterflies in his stomach started to turn..

"I'd like that Tim, thank you." Jenni smiled back, for she was nervous too. She had never had the feelings of love before. She had never dated anyone in her life.

They made their way back to Tim's trailer. With the quake, things were still a mess inside. He was able to get the foundation stands back in place underneath.

"I was able to get the water lines back on, but the gas company can't come till next week with everything that has happened." Tim said as he cleared off his recliner.

"So, no hot shower?" Jenni jested with a smile as she walked into the kitchen.

"No, but you can use my bed to sleep in. I'll sleep here on the recliner." Tim said as he continued to pick things up. Jenni sauntered over to him. Tim stood up after picking up a picture that had fallen. She grabbed him and kissed him. Tim dropped the picture and embraced her, placing his hands in the small of her back, pulling her into his waist as the kiss deepened. They made their way to his bedroom, kissing and removing their clothes. It was the most passion either had ever felt. They made love till the early morning, finally falling asleep in each other's arms.

CHAPTER 23

FREEDOM

After meeting with Chief Red Cloud, Dr. Underwood was taken to a trailer at the sacred circle where he would stay for his research. The next morning when he woke, Samuel was sitting in a chair in the corner of his room.

"Morning, doctor." Samuel said, reading the morning paper.

"What are you?" Dr. Underwood was startled by his presence.

"Listen, doctor, I'm your benefactor in your new research. Come on, get dressed. Let's see what you can help us with." Samuel put down the paper and got up to go outside.

Dr. Underwood got dressed and came out as he was amazed to see the Tesla theories at work. Then he saw the young man in the circle.

"So, who is this?" Dr. Underwood was shaken to see.

"My son, Dr. Underwood. And this is Dr. McFadden, the head of our research team." Samuel gestured with his left hand to Dr. McFadden.

"Yes, yes Dr. McFadden, leading authority on mythology and language professor at Cambridge." Dr. Underwood was delighted to see her.

"Dr. Underwood, we need your help, controlling the power that his son generates when he is in full form." Dr. McFadden showed him a computer tablet.

"Full form?" He was confused by her remark.

"His son is the Thunderbird, controlled by the harness, he wears." She said, trying to catch him up to speed.

"Oh, yes, the tattoo. It's a harness. It became a part of him. Only by death can it be removed." His geared intellect was now turning with excitement.

"Yes, doctor. But I don't want him to die. I want to harness his power, control it." Samuel said, giving him a serious look.

"The lightning... you have set up already. With the coils. You need to focus the wave, like they do with the... like the <u>lithotrispy</u> treatment." Dr. Underwood was fidgeting with his hands as he explained.

"Kidney stones?" Dr. McFadden said with disgust.

"Yes, yes, exactly. By controlling the depth of the waves. You can move it or sustain it." He became more excited in his rambling.

"And how do we do that doctor?" Samuel asked with delight for a new concept.

"I'll show you." Just, as Dr. Underwood moved to the circle Jeromia woke, scrambling to his feet. Dr. Underwood froze. There was a movement on a nearby cliff as Samuel took notice. He motioned to George and Lou to check it out. The two moved quickly to the van and drove off.

"Easy, doctor, he cannot harm you unless you go into the circle. The wards around the circle keep him caged, but the quakes, they must stop." Samuel warned, taking a step to grab him if he went too far.

"Yes, yes, absolutely. But then why the necklace?" His mind was running at full speed now.

"There are others like him, those who would try to stop me. As long as you wear that, they cannot see. Give me a list of what you need, and my men will get it." Samuel said, now more relaxed that the good doctor didn't wander too far.

"Yes, yes, right away." Dr. Underwood ran back to the trailer to grab a notepad.

Agents Greene and Folsome scrambled from the cliff to get back to their car. George and Lou pulled up to the agents' car and saw the two agents approaching. George stopped the van between them and the car. Lou got out and held an AR-15 pointing right at the two agents, Greene and Folsome froze with their hands in the air.

"We are with the FBI!" Agent Folsome said. George got out with his pistol pointing at the two agents.

"On the ground, hands behind your back." Lou said, George approached gun still raised at the two agents.

The two men lay on the ground. Suddenly Nakoma appeared on the hill, seeing what was going on. Nakoma looked right at George and Lou. She appeared in front of George snatching him up and throwing him back into the van. Pain struck her as she touched him.

"*Wards*!" Nakoma thought as Lou opened fire. She disappeared and reappeared behind him, running him through with her spear. Lou cried out in pain and slumped over, dropping the rifle. Agents Greene and Folsome scrambled to their feet, drawing their weapons at George. He began to get up, and then Nakoma walked around the van, now holding the blood-soaked spear.

"Stay back. He's mine." Nakoma said to the two agents. George went to aim at her with his gun, but Nakoma ran her spear into his right shoulder. He groaned in pain, dropping the pistol. She pulled the spear out ready to strike again.

"Wait!" Agent Folsome said, still pointing the gun in her direction..

"He killed my father. He will pay in our ways on our lands." Nakoma said as the rage consumed her.

George got up, clenching his shoulder, head held high. Nakoma ran her spear into his gut, driving it through till it came out his back. George fell to his knees. Then a Native war club appeared in her hand as she walked behind him.

"For my family, my friend!" Nakoma struck George in the back of the head with such force his eyes popped out, and blood flew from his mouth. He lay on the ground, lifeless. Agent Greene and Folsome held their weapons on Nakoma now as she looked up.

"Wait. Red Cloud is the one you want, not me!" Nakoma said as turned toward them war club in her hand dripping in blood.

"What are you? Who are you?" Agent Folsome said as his hands shook in fear of what he was seeing.

"A guardian. Please put down your guns. Red Cloud is on the other side.' Nakoma gestured to the other side of the ridge. Nakoma vanished at the top of the ridge, looking down. And then she reappeared back in front of them. The agents were startled by what they were seeing.

"The wards around him. I can't get to him." She said looking now at the two.

"You take care of his men. We'll get the wards down." Greene said, holstering his weapon. Folsome holstered his weapon as well, and now ran to check on the two dead men. He then took the necklaces off of them, putting one on and taking the other one to Agent Greene. David just looked at it.

"That will only protect you from my site. Do you wish me harm?" Nakoma said, looking at the two men ready to defend herself.

"No, but we do want better answers." Greene said, looking at Nakoma.

"Take their van. Once I have handled the guards, you two break the wards around the circle." She commanded in her ghostly voice.

"We want Red Cloud alive, guardian." Greene said as he and Folsome made their way to the van.

"Call me Spirit Walker, but he will answer for my parents' deaths and the death of my friend." Nakoma said, turning away from them.

"He will, but we need him to answer questions." Agent Greene said not sure he could trust her. Nakoma went over to George's body and retrieved the Spear, turning into a bow and arrows appeared on her back.

"I promise you. Free Jeromia, and I may let him live."

She vanished and then appeared near the circle, bow drawn. Security came at her as the scientists scrambled to run away. She fired a shot, hitting the first guard in the leg. Then she spun around on one knee and hit another. Then she vanished again, appearing behind another, hitting him with an arrow. Two guards remained, and they were standing next to Samuel. He was in range as Nakoma took aim with two arrows drawn, she released the arrows and the two guards dropped dead.

Agents Greene and Folsome drove up approaching near the circle. Jeromia was in shock seeing Nakoma appear, her killing the guards, and the van pulling in. Folsome ran to the circle.

"It's okay. We're here to get you out." Folsome said, looking around to find a way to help him escape.

"The wards, you have to break the wards." Jeromia said, pointing to the symbols on the ground. Nakoma walked toward Samuel, changing the bow into the war club. Samuel pulled his gun. Before he could raise it, Nakoma was upon him, hitting his hand with the gun. Then she hit him in the right knee, dropping him to the ground.

"Nakoma wait. Don't do it!" Jeromia said, pleading with her not to kill him. Agent Greene turned toward the two.

"We need him Spirit Walker." Greene shouted moving toward her.

"You cannot touch me special agent." Samuel said, grimacing in pain. Folsome started breaking the wards, and Jeromia turned into the Thunderbird. Folsome fell backward in terror, scrambling to get away. Greene ran toward Nakoma and Samuel. The Thunderbird stepped through the barrier, screaming in pain from the wards. Lightning filled the air, and thunder shook the ground. He was free at last. He flew up into the air, hovering over the circle. Everyone looked up at him except Samuel.

He scrambled away to his car. Nakoma then turned her club into a spear and shield, ready for the Thunderbird to strike. The Thunderbird screamed as lightning and thunder filled the skies. Agents Greene and Folsome saw Dr. Underwood hiding behind some equipment. They rushed to grab him. Dr. McFadden moved from where she was hiding and helped Samuel into the passenger seat of his car.

"Drive fast." Samuel said, still holding his hand in pain.

"What about Underwood?" McFadden said as she started the car to drive off.

"He told us what we needed. Now drive." Samuel ordered, and McFadden sped away.

The Thunderbird flew off, and Nakoma relaxed. Now looking at the two agents, and Dr. Underwood.

"Take the necklace off." She said in her ghostly voice. Dr. Underwood took the necklace off in fear and threw it onto the ground.

"Red Cloud got away. But we got four scientists, and a lot of evidence." Agent Greene said as it wasn't a total loss. Just then three of the scientists' heads exploded, and their bodies fell to the ground.

"One scientist, a lot of evidence." Folsome said to try to lighten the mood.

"You need to go now. Red Cloud we'll find you." Nakoma said as she turned to walk to the circle.

"We have questions for you, Spirit Walker." Greene said sternly not wanting to let her go.

"I'm here to help. Concern yourselves with Red Cloud and not me." Nakoma vanished leaving them behind.

"That was the Spirit Walker?" Dr. Underwood asked with new delight in his curiosity.

"Yes, you know of her?" Greene said, now looking at him. Dr. Underwood nodded his head.

"Good. Get in the van. You're coming with us." Folsome said grabbing him by the arm and escorting him to the van.

CHAPTER 24

THE FIGHT

Nakoma appeared in the spirit world, focusing now on the Thunderbird. He was moving quickly to the north. He landed in front of a mansion in the woods. He transformed back into Jeromia, stumbling his way through the front door and entering the home. The inside was beautiful, with vaulted ceilings and a country feel. Heads of many animals were along the fireplace wall. A bear hide rug lie in front of the fireplace surrounded by two couches. Jeromia made his way up to the stairs to his room, where he fell into the bed, fast asleep. Nakoma was at ease knowing he was safe. She then appeared back at Tim's trailer. Ms. Kern and Tim were sitting, writing things on paper at the table.

"Nakoma! You have to stop doing that." Tim and Jenni were startled by her appearing.

"Sorry, Tim. We have to get you somewhere safe." Nakoma said with urgency in her voice.

"Funny you say that. I was telling Tim, there's a job opening for a fire chief in Golden." Jenni replied, looking at Tim. Nakoma's look was anger, and then she relaxed and thought.

"Yes, that would be best." She said staring at the two of them.

"Nakoma, could you turn..." Tim was gesturing to her outfit that was still making them uneasy. Nakoma removed the head dress turning it back into a bracelet and placing it on her wrist. She was back in her normal clothing.

"Thank you, Nakoma. I know I can't tell you how to live your life, or even try to understand what you're going through." He didn't know how to tell her.

"What Tim is trying to say is it's okay. And you will always be welcome wherever he is." Jenni added with a smile.

"I know. Part of my curse is empathy. And how one feels. I think I'm in love with Jeromia. Not really sure but I feel drawn to him in some way. I like the way he looked at me when we met." Nakoma said searching within her heart.

"Follow your heart. I will not fault you for it." Tim said grabbing Jenni's hand.

"I can since you're a good woman. And you care for him. I must go and figure out how to reach him." Nakoma said as she looked at the two of them, realizing that he was not alone. It bothered her, though not seeing a place for her with them.

"Thank you, Nakoma, and be careful." Tim said. He didn't know how to help, or even give advice into what she had to do.

"You too!" Nakoma understood his feelings. Nakoma put the headdress back on, vanished, and appeared at Pete's home. Pete saw a flash and looked out his window.

"Nakoma!" Pete ran to the door and went outside.

"Come, we have work to do." She stood waiting for Pete to get to her. Pete walked up to her, and Nakoma grabbed his arm. They vanished and appeared on the cliff by the sacred circle.

"He's already cleaned it up." Nakoma said, looking down at the sacred circle.

"Cleaned up what?" Pete was confused, but excited that he got to teleport.

"Never mind! I want to try something." Nakoma came up to Pete, placing her hands on either side of his head. She closed her eyes focusing on his thoughts. Pete closed his, eyes, puckering his lips for her kiss. Suddenly, they were standing in a room filled with things all around from his happiness to his sadness, like a holographic image in his mind. Nakoma opened her eyes, saw Pete puckered up and slapped him on the chest.

"Where are we in your head, Pete? What is all this?" Nakoma said, trying to get him to focus on the surroundings.

"My memories I guess. This is the poster I got at the first Comic Con in Vegas. And this..." Pete began to walk around, totally amazed to be walking around in his own head.

"I get it. What about that box? It's dark and filled with pain." Nakoma pointed to a box covered in shadow. The box was dark and looked like an old chest. It was the largest thing there. Nakoma touched the box, and Pete began to cry, falling into the fetal position.

"Sorry, Pete!" Nakoma let go of the link. They were standing on the ridge again. "I know now what I must do." Then Nakoma teleported them back to his place. She left him again. Pete stood there in awkwardness. She appeared at the mansion, removing the headdress and knocking on the door. A minute later, Jeromia answered. She grabbed him and kissed him. They kissed in the doorway for several minutes, and then Nakoma pulled back, looking at him.

"Come in!" Jeromia said as he grabbed her hand. Nakoma went inside, and he offered her a seat on the couch.

"I'm here to help, Jeromia, but I can't fight the feelings I have for you." Her love for him was uncontrollable.

"I love you. I mean, yeah, I love you. I love you. I mean, yeah" Jeromia proclaimed pulling her to his lap with ease.

"I love you too, Jeromia." They began to make out there on the couch as Samuel pulled into the driveway, making his way to the front door. Nakoma and Jeromia did not hear him come in. Samuel dropped his keys in the tray next to the door, as he saw the two. Both of them jumped up.

"Welcome home, son. And who is our guest?" Samuel said with a sear of hate, already knowing who she was. Jeremiah rushed to tackle his father. He took him to the ground, and Nakoma put her headdress on as Jeromia turned into the Thunderbird. He grabbed his father, throwing him through the front bay window. Samuel landed fifty feet away on the ground, not moving. The Thunderbird climbed out the window, walking to Samuel.

"Jeromia, stop!" Nakoma cried out. Then the Thunderbird turned toward her and screamed to the sky. Clouds rolled in with thunder and lightning. Nakoma then made her shield and spear appear, jumping out the window.

"Hear me, Jeromia. You have to fight this. You take control." Nakoma pleaded to Jeromia, but the monster was in control now.

The Thunderbird sent a lightning bolt at her. She blocked with her shield, and it knocked her off her feet. She sprang back up planting her feet this time.

"Channel the lightning Nakoma!" She said to herself. The Thunderbird sent another bolt at her. This time she was ready. The lightning hit the shield. As she touched the spear to it and, while spinning, pointed the spear back at him. The lightning flew from the spear back at him hitting him square in the chest, knocking him back on to the ground about twenty feet. He sprang to his feet, taking flight. He then dove in on her fast. Nakoma side stepped as the Thunderbird hit the ground, creating a quack of thunder. Nakoma fell again, scrambling to get to her feet.

"Jeromia, stop. I love you." She pleaded some more, not knowing how to reach him.

The Thunderbird rushed in, sending lightning bolts and punching the ground. Nakoma vanished, and then re-appeared behind him with the war club. She Struck the Thunderbird in the lower back. He planted his talons into the ground, spinning with his wings, catching Nakoma's shield and knocking her back onto the ground. She sprang up again.

"Jeromia, please, I beg you." She tried again, trying to reach the one she loved.

The Thunderbird screamed again, this time unleashing lightning all around. Nakoma moved over to Samuel's body with her shield over them and planted her spear. Several lightning bolts hit the shield. She touched the spear to the shield and delivered it back at the Thunderbird. Lightning struck him so hard that, it shoved him into the side of the mansion. He stood there hulked over with rage.

"I'm sorry, Jeromia!" Then Nakoma teleported in front of him, with the war club. Sending a crushing blow to his face. The Thunderbird collapsed unconscious from the strike, and Nakoma wept.

"I'm sorry!" Nakoma began to cry. Then she looked back at Samuel still lying unconscious on the ground. She touched the Thunderbird, teleporting them to the spirit world. There, she waited for him to wake.

CHAPTER 25

SEPARATION

Nakoma sat next to Jeromia, by the stream in the spirit world. Bob the cat came and sat on her lap.

"Spirit Walker, why have you brought him here?" GES said with concern on her face.

"I love him!" Nakoma said as she wept by his side.

"You cannot control the Thunderbird." GES looked at her with sadness.

"But he can. I know he can." Nakoma looked at her with tears in her eyes. She had to believe there was hope.

"Maybe, maybe not. It's a risk that could cost you both your lives." GES knew Nakoma's love was strong. Could it be strong enough for the both of them?

"I have to try." Nakoma said as she stood to face GES.

"Only by the pool at the tree, can this be done, nowhere else. But you could lose yourself, your life. Moreover, you could lose him." GES warned with a heavy heart.

"Like I said, I have to try. I will help him, GES." She stood firm, looking at GES with determination.

"Okay then. I will go make preparations." GES vanished leaving them there with Bob.

"Thank you." Nakoma said, holding Bob in her arms. Then Jeromia came to, startled by his whereabouts.

"It's okay, Jeromia, you're safe." Nakoma rushed to his side. Bob the cat came up and jumped into his lap. Jeromia stroked his fur and smiled.

"Where are we?" Jeromia was looking around, unsure of what to make of all of it.

"In the spirit world." Nakoma just kind of laughed, for she had felt like that at first too.

"What are all these blue lights with smoke trails?" Jeromia tried to poke one of the orbs as it passed by.

"Spirits of the past." Nakoma continued to laugh at him and his amazement.

"This place is cool." Jeromia got to his feet continuing to take it all in.

"I think so, too, now." She smiled as she grabbed his hand with hers.

"What do you mean 'now'?" Jeromia asked, not understanding what was not to like.

"At first, I was scared of what was happening. But I accepted it and became the Spirit Walker." Nakoma said pulling him to her.

"I can't control this Nakoma." Jeromia was scared of his fate and what it would mean for them.

"Yes, you can, and I will help you." Nakoma looked into his eyes, longing for a kiss.

"How?" He was not sure of what she meant, now looking into her eyes.

"Like Spock's mind meld or Xavier's mind powers." Nakoma said with sarcasm and a giggle. Jeromia kissed her and, then pulled away just enough.

"I believe you." The two made love there on the side of the stream for several hours. Finally, both of them fell asleep. When they awoke, GES appeared.

"Morning." GES said, standing over their naked bodies, with a look of disappointment. "Did you two get it out of your systems? We have work to do."

"Who are you?" Jeromia said, trying to get his clothes to cover himself.

"I am GES, the Great Elder Spirit and you're Jeromia, the Thunderbird. Nakoma is going to help you take control of your power. Come now, everything is ready."

"We're gonna walk, GES. I want him to see it all." Nakoma said with a gesture to go away so they could get dressed.

"Very well. We'll walk." GES just laughed as she turned her back to give them some sort of privacy.

"GES, go!" Nakoma shouted, now mad that she wouldn't give them space.

"No more hanky-panky for you two." GES turned to give them a serious look of importance. "I'll see you there." She vanished, leaving them to get ready.

"Crazy old lady, huh!" Jeromia replied, thinking a least it wasn't the first time he had been walked in on.

"Yes, but she's right. Let's go." Nakoma got up, getting dressed. Jeromia just stared for a moment. She was so beautiful. Nakoma looked back at him and smiled.

"Come on lovebird." It was just something she said, but she also liked it. She laughed to her self-realizing that it was her nick name now for him. The two got dressed and made their way to the ridge overlooking the valley.

"Whoa, this is amazing, Nakoma." He stood in amazement looking into the valley. He could see all of it's beauty as it glowed in the special hue of blue.

"See that tree? That's where we're going. You ready?" Nakoma took his hand and focused on the tree.

"Yeah!" Just then they teleported to the entrance of the tree. "Wow, how did you do that? This thing is enormous."

Nakoma went into the tree. Jeromia was close behind. She made her way to the pool. The stone path rose from the pool, as she walked to the center.

"Come on now." Nakoma said, looking back at him as he took it all in. They made their way to the pool. The stones rose, creating the path to the center. Jeromia followed her to the center of the pool. Nakoma turned around, taking both of his hands into hers. "Do you trust me?"

"Yes, Nakoma." Jeromia was now looking into her eyes.

"You need to fight. Take control when we find it. Can you do that?" Nakoma was serious as she looked at him.

"But..." Jeromia was now not sure of what was about to happen.

"You can do this. Your spirit is stronger than his. I'll be there with you." Nakoma said, trying to give him the confidence to face his fears.

"Okay, I'll do it. I love you." Jeromia pulled her to him.

"I love you!" The two kissed and embraced. Nakoma placed her hands on the side of his head. Vines came down out of the tree, encasing them into a cocoon. They were now in his mind. There were clouds with thunder and lightning all around them. Jeromia was scared and holding on tightly to Nakoma's hand.

"Calm down, Jeromia. We need to find him. I'm here with you." Jeromia took several deep breaths and let go of Nakoma's hand.

'Okay, let's do it." Jeromia was now showing some confidence.

"There should be like a box or chest or a door where you're keeping your fears." Nakoma was searching the area. "Or a cave!" Just then they were looking upon a cave and a huge one at that.

"Or yes, a cave!" Jeromia now was not so sure. Nakoma readied her shield and spear.

"Do I need weapons?" Jeromia said, looking at her and not knowing what to do.

"It's your mind, Jeromia." The Thunderbird came out of the cave. He was larger now about three stories high and screaming as he came out. Suddenly, the Thunderbird threw lightning at Nakoma. She blocked the strike with her shield, but the force was too great. She was knocked off her feet, and the shield fell into the darkness. Jeromia stood in shock as he saw her get blasted. The Thunderbird came at Jeromia, swinging his fist. Jeromia dodged the blows.

"This is your mind, Jeromia. Fight back! He's using your power." Nakoma said as she got to her feet.

"My power, my power, my power, *my power!*" Jeromia now stood ready to face his fear.

"Now, Jeromia!" Nakoma said as she was thinking of another way to help. The Thunderbird screamed with a thunderous force, reaching deep with his lightning striking. Jeromia stood ready as the Thunderbird unleashed a mighty thunderbolt at him. Jeromia did not move. He caught the thunderbolt and held it in his hands, toying with it like a new ball he just unwrapped. He smiled and then, with a quick push, sent it back at the Thunderbird. The bolt struck the Thunderbird, knocking him back into the cavernous rock face. The Thunderbird dropped to one knee, screaming at Jeromia.

Nakoma began to stab spears into the area around her, wide enough to have the Thunderbird stand in the middle. Nakoma then shot arrows at the Thunderbird, to get its attention.

"Get him into the center!" She screamed trying to lure him in. The Thunderbird came at her. Jeromia moved to the center of the circle to block him. The Thunderbird swung at Jeromia. He caught the mighty fist, as it drove him to one knee. Nakoma began to throw bolas with copper mesh lines around his feet and arms, tying them off to the spears. Jeromia stood holding the fist, of the Thunderbird. Nakoma touched one of the spears, causing the lines to tighten and hold the Thunderbird in place.

"Now, Jeromia. It's your power!" Nakoma yelled again, ready for Jeromia to take his shot.

Jeremiah could feel the lightning forming from his toes to his hands, and his eyes began to glow red. He moved to the middle to face the Thunderbird in the center. He reached and grabbed the stone in the center of the Thunderbird's chest, releasing the lightning. There was a loud explosion in a flash of light so forceful it knocked Nakoma back down. Smoke filled the area. As it settled, Nakoma could see Jeromia standing in the center, changed and powerful. His wings were huge and beautiful. His head was held high, looking like an angel. There were bracers and armbands of gold on each arm, he wore a loincloth with a belt, and his feet were more like that of an eagle. He stood there now looking at his hands. The cowl on his head was that of a mighty bird.

"Jeromia, is that you?" Nakoma got to her feet, dusting herself off. He looked at her and smiled.

"Yes, it is me, Nakoma" She rushed to his arms and they kissed. As he embraced her, the cocoon fell apart and there they stood in the center of the pool kissing.

"Ahem... Spirit Walker." Nakoma and Jeromia stood smiling at one another in GES's displeasure.

"This is the sacred pool you two." GES said with a gesture to get out.

"And love is sacred to GES." Nakoma teleported them both to his home. Samuel still lay on the ground unconscious.

"How did you do that with time?" Jeromia was shocked to return to when they left.

"I have to focus, but I can only go back to the last moment I was in. I need you to take the necklace off of him for me."

"You're not going to kill him now?" Jeromia looked at her with concern.

"No, but I'm going to give him to the FBI for questioning." Nakoma said, moving back a little, still holding his hands.

"I'm sorry. He killed your folks." Jeromia now felt remorse for what his father had done.

"You don't have to apologize, my lovebird." Nakoma touched his face and looked into his eyes. Jeromia went over to his father and removed the necklace. Just then, Samuel woke.

"He's all yours, Spirit Walker." Jeromia said as he backed away from his father. Samuel scrambled to get to his feet, reaching for his gun that was not even there.

"Don't worry. I'll be gentle." Nakoma grabbed him, teleporting him to the FBI office in downtown Denver. There, agents Greene and Folsome were interrogating Dr. Underwood.

"I need to speak to agents Greene or Folsome." Nakoma said, holding Chief Red Cloud now in an arm bar. Samuel stood silent as Agent Folsome came into the room.

"Chief Red Cloud, how nice of you to join us. Spirit Walker, thank you for the assist. Would you be sticking around for a bit?"

"Not at this time Agent Folsome, but the Thunderbird has been controlled."

"As you wish, and thanks again." Folsome came and put handcuffs on Samuel, ready to escort him back to an interrogation room. Nakoma teleported back to Jeromia.

CHAPTER 26

PARTNERS FOR NOW

By the next morning, there was a knock at the door of Jeromia's house.

"Wake up, someone's here." Nakoma said, trying to wake Jeromia.

"All right, I'm up." Jeromia came downstairs, seeing two men standing in the broken living room. "Can I help you, gentlemen?" Their faces were in shock at, seeing Jeromia.

'Where's your father, Jeromia?"

"He won't be back for a while. Is there anything I can help you with?" Jeromia made his way over to them.

"No, no, just wanted to welcome him home, is all. Can we get a crew for your home? Repairs are needed, I see."

"What is your name, brother?" He asked looking at both men.

"Isaiah Running Bear!"

"Then yes, Isaiah, send a crew to repair." Nakoma came to the top of the banister wearing nothing but a T-shirt. The two men just stared.

"And what is your name, brother?" Jeromia asked, now getting angry with them.

"James Stone Wolf."

"You'd both be wise to keep your eyes off my woman. Now leave before I change my mind." Jeromia threatened, and the two men left quickly.

"Your woman!" Nakoma said with a smile, leaning on the banister.

"Yeah, my woman." He said with a smile, rushing back up the stairs.

"Silly lovebird, come back to bed."

That morning in the FBI office in Denver. Agents Greene and Folsome were questioning Samuel. Director Jennings knocked on the door. "Can I have a word with you two?" Greene and Folsome came into the hallway.

"This just came from the secretary of state. It releases Samuel Red Cloud of any and all charges. It has labeled him as an asset to the State Department." The director handed Greene a release order.

"You're kidding, right? He's a murderer." Folsome said as Greene looked at the order.

"Orders Agent Folsome." The director stood, just as upset with what had come down the chain.

"You know this is wrong, director!" Greene said, throwing the paper on the floor.

"I get it, I do, but we have to release him." Agent Greene flung open the door looking at Samuel.

"You're free to go." Samuel got up and walked out of the room. He turned around as he passed the three men.

"I'll be needing Dr. Underwood now. He's part of my team." Samuel said with a smile. Director Jennings turned and looked at Folsome.

"This has to be a joke." Folsome said, turning to go get Dr. Underwood. Dr. Underwood followed agent Folsome to where Samuel was standing.

"Come along, doctor." Samuel said, motioning with his hand.

"I'm free to go?" Dr. Underwood replied in disbelief.

"Yes, doctor. Come now, we must leave." Dr. Underwood followed Samuel out of the building. There was a limousine waiting for them. The driver held open the door. Samuel got in, and then Dr. Underwood followed. A man sat across from them in the limo. The driver shut the door.

"We pay you to be discreet, Chief Red Cloud."

"There are things in play that none of us can control. I have found two of them thus far." Samuel got comfortable in his seat.

"You have proved the fables to be true, but we seek control Chief Red Cloud. We are paying you to figure it out."

"In due time. My son will come around and be ready for what you need. As far as the other one, she will be under our control." Samuel said, tapping on the glass of the window next to him.

"And how do you plan to control the Spirit Walker?"

"Love!" Samuel smiled after he said this.

"We expect results. We will drop you off at the airport. Any ideas on where you go next?"

"Juarez, Mexico!" Samuel said, leaving the intrigue in the air.

"Okay, report in a week once you've landed."

"Will do. Got any scotch?" Samuel leaned forward.

"Here you go."

"Cheers." Samuel said as he held up his glass in a toast.

"Who are you?" Dr. Underwood said, confused to what was going on.

"Secretary of State Gary Thorn. I'm the one paying Samuel here and making sure we have no other loose ends."

"You're a friend then?" Dr. Underwood felt more at ease.

"Partners for now." Mr. Thorn said with the look that said it was only business.

CHAPTER 27

ANOTHER DREAM

Tim and Jenni moved most of what he had left in to their two vehicles, and drove to Golden, Colorado. Tim stayed with Jenni until his interview with the department. He got the job hands down, with his track record of experience. That night Nakoma appeared at the station,

"Settling in?"

"Yes, thank you." Tim didn't seem to jump when she appeared.

"I think she's good for you." Nakoma said with a smile.

"You do, do you?" Tim replied with a smirk as he looked through some paperwork.

"Yes, she's driven, and she can see a good man." Nakoma moved to the doorway to his office, looking to see if anyone else was there.

"Thanks. There's an extra cot here if you need." Tim pointed to the corner of his room.

"I'm good, but I wanted to say thanks for everything." Nakoma turned to face him.

"No problem, kid. Hey, where's Bob?" Tim said with a curious thought as he smiled at her.

"Why do you want him." Nakoma looked surprised but some what glad.

"I kind of do miss him?" Nakoma vanished and then reappeared with Bob. She handed him over to Tim.

"It's not good for him to stay in the spirit world." Nakoma smiled, knowing Bob would have a good home.

"Thanks, Nakoma." Tim held him, stroking his fur and Bob just lapped it up.

"She is good for you. Don't mess it up." Nakoma chuckled seeing the two of them together.

"I won't, be careful" Nakoma winked and vanished. "Welcome to your new home, Bob."

That night as Nakoma and Jeromia slept a dream came over her in the early hours in the morning. She was walking with what appeared to be an alleyway. The stench of garbage and fumes from the sewer lines, turned her stomach. Rats crossed her path and sounds of dogs barking filled the air. Then she spotted a blood trail. She followed it until she heard the sounds of something eating. As she approached, she caught a shadow on the side of a building, feasting on something. Nakoma turned the corner, and there it was. It was small, with what appeared to be like a wretched looking dog, but it sat on its hind legs like a man. His skin was black, and its arms were tearing into a body and eating the innards. Then the dead body looked up and reached toward Nakoma.

"Help... me!..." He cried to her.

The creature turned and faced Nakoma. Its face was like a gargoyle, eyes glowing green like a cat. It hissed at her like a snake, blood dripping from its fingertips. Then the creature vanished, appearing behind her and striking with his claws. Nakoma screamed in pain, turning to face him, but he was gone. He appeared again by her side, striking her leg. She fell as the creature climbed on top of her. looking at her face.

"Spirit Walker!" The creature said. Then the creature lunged for her throat. Nakoma screamed.

"Nakoma, Nakoma! I'm here Nakoma." Jeromia said, trying to wake her up. Nakoma flew up out of bed.

"Where is he?" Nakoma was searching for the creature.

"Where's who?" Jeromia got up, trying to comfort her.

"The creature." She looked all around the room.

"It's just us, Nakoma." Jeremiah saw her leg. "How did this happen? You're bleeding."

"I don't know. It's like I was there with him. He was feeding on someone and then he saw me. He attacked me." Nakoma was scared, not knowing what was going on.

"But it was a dream, right?" Jeromia moved to hold her, but she moved away.

"Yeah, but it was real. I was there." She began to panic.

"Come, let's get you patched up." Jeromia helped her to the bathroom to mend her wounds.

Weeks went by as Nakoma and Jeromia returned to their respective schools. She finished out her senior year, making it as the valedictorian. Though most of the school was destroyed, they decided to have the graduation in tents in front of the school. Her class was small with only eighty-nine students total. Nakoma turned eighteen two days after graduation. Jeromia was soon to be twenty. Jeromia led the team of Colorado University in sacks, giving the team a shot at a bowl year. Every night they spent in his father's house, and every night the dreams returned. Nakoma tried to focus on her life with Jeromia, but the reality of her responsibilities outweighed everything. One night, Nakoma and Jeromia sat by the fireplace.

"So, what are you going to do?" Jeromia said, looking into her face, knowing that life as they knew it was about to take a turn.

"Now, hopefully start next year at CU." Nakoma said with optimism.

"No, the dreams!" Jeromia smiled pulling her in close.

"I have to go to Mexico." She said, looking into his face with regret.

"Is that where the creature is?" Jeromia said, now eager to support her.

"Yes. It says here on the global news that thirty-nine people are dead from brutal attacks." Nakoma pulled up the news on her phone and showed him.

"I can come with you." He wanted to be by her side.

"No, sorry, but you won't be much help in this." Nakoma shot him down, trying to keep him safe.

"So, I'm supposed just live the college dream and let the love of my life go off and fight something that we don't even know what it is?" Jeromia was upset, shifting his body away from her.

"Sorry lovebird. But I need to go, and besides, my father said you have to win a national championship." She was trying to make him laugh a little.

"You know I don't like this." Jeromia got up and moved to the fireplace.

"I'll be fine. Anyways, your called to do you protect the lands, and I stop all the other things that go bump in the night." Nakoma said sarcastically, trying to get him to relax.

"Okay, Nakoma!" Jeromia threw another log onto the fire.

"Thank you, love-bird!" Nakoma walked over to him. Nakoma and Jeromia kissed as the evening faded.

EPILOGUE

GES walked up to Nakoma's horse, tying a feather, and a small spirit stone into his mane. She bowed her head as she touched him. Instantly, they were in a forest. She looked up to the horse and smiled. The horse ran, venturing into his new surroundings. GES then teleported back to the spirit world to the great tree. She approached the pool in the center. The stones rose making a path to the center. GES made her way to the center and stood looking up at the stone.

"The seer is ready to wake." Gaia said to her as the glow of the stone changed for a second to a bright red.

"Fabiana to grows strong, yes, but so young they are, to today's world." GES pondered, looking at the stone.

"She will be needed for what's to come. Do not fear GES, for these to be chosen are strong." Gaia said, knowing GES had compassion for the girls.

"Yes, Mother Gaia. Fate will always be the way and our hope to protect what is." GES sat in the center like a monk priest and went into deep meditation.

NOTE FROM THE AUTHOR

I would like to give thanks to God, my family, and friends. It has been a great learning experience in writing for me. I have played role playing games for most of my life, creating narratives for my characters and growing in their experiences. I have served in the US military, and I am proud of the heritage for the American nation I served. I got the ideas to write when my daughter was struggling in school. I wanted to create something that would inspire her along with other young people to read. I chose Nakoma because she is someone who can be a light to young women today. I have had the privilege to read many fantasy books or fiction. My greatest influences are R. A. Salvatore, Anne Rice, and Robert Patterson. Though I'm new to this. I hope you will find my stories entertaining. Special thanks to the team at Palmetto Publishing.